DEA

"It just hasn't been that great a day," said Mike.

"Well, let's start making it better," said Joy.

She opened her bag, and Mike knew she was getting the gin. As usual, she didn't seem at all worried that some adult might see them. They could get in trouble. He looked around the empty school parking lot.

She pulled out the silver flask. It shone in the late afternoon sunlight.

"Go ahead. Drink."

Mike was surprised at how much he wanted it. He glanced around once more, then uncapped the top and took a swig.

A sweet warmth tingled through his body. He smiled.

"See, I told you I'd make it better," Joy said. "Let's get out of here."

They climbed into Mike's Mustang. As he pulled out, Joy turned to him and smiled. "Now I'm going to teach you some *real* exciting games . . ."

•

NOW OPEN!
THE NIGHT OWL CLUB

Pool Tables, Video Games, Great Munchies,
Dance Floor, Juke Box, *Live* Bands On Weekend.

* * *

Bring A Date Or Come Alone . . .

* * *

Students From Cooper High School,
Hudson Military Academy,
Cooper Riding Academy for Girls
Especially Welcome . . .

* * *

Located Just Outside Of Town.
Take Thirteen Bends Road,
Or Follow Path Through Woods.

* * *

Don't Let The Dark Scare You Away . . .

* * *

Jake and Jenny Demos proprietors
Teen club, no alcohol served.

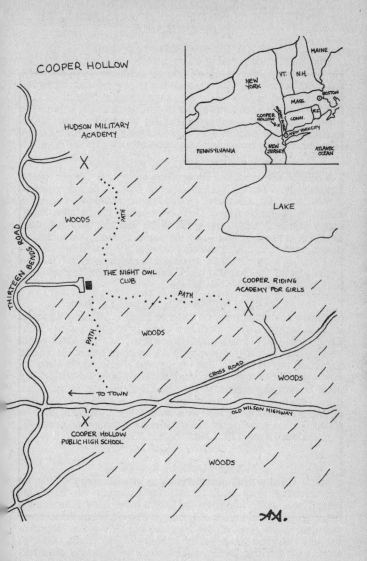

COOPER HOLLOW

MAINE

NEW
YORK
VT. N.H.

BOSTON
MASS.

COOPER
HOLLOW
CONN.

NEW YORK CITY

PENNSYLVANIA

NEW
JERSEY

ATLANTIC
OCEAN

HUDSON MILITARY
ACADEMY

LAKE

WOODS

PATH

THIRTEEN BENDS ROAD

THE NIGHT OWL
CLUB

COOPER RIDING
ACADEMY FOR GIRLS

PATH

PATH

WOODS

WOODS

CROSS ROAD

TO TOWN

OLD WILSON HIGHWAY

COOPER HOLLOW
PUBLIC HIGH SCHOOL

WOODS

THE NIGHTMARE CLUB SERIES
INVITES YOU TO ENTER . . . AT YOUR OWN RISK!
NOW AVAILABLE

#1 JOY RIDE by Richard Lee Byers

Mike doesn't see anything wrong with his drinking and driving. He thinks he's totally in control. But his girlfriend Karen knows he has a problem. Then Mike meets a pretty new girl in a slinky red dress at the Night Owl Club. Joy doesn't mind if Mike drinks. In fact, she encourages him to drink—and then to get behind the wheel. Mike doesn't know it yet, but Joy is a deadly ghost. Killed by a drunk driver decades ago, she has come back for one reason—to get her revenge by helping Mike drive himself over the edge . . .

#2 THE INITIATION by Nick Baron

Kimberly Kilpatrick will do anything to fit in at Cooper Riding Academy. So when the hottest clique in the girls' boarding school invites her to join, Kimberly's ready to prove she belongs—even if it means losing her boyfriend, Griff, who doesn't like her new, "bad" image. Kimberly thinks the group is the best . . . until kids start drowning in a nearby lake—and she begins dreaming about a murderous water spirit with a sinister hold over her new friends. Somehow Kimberly must resist its horrible demands before Griff is lured to the edge of the churning black waters . . . where he could lose his life—and she could lose her soul.

#3 WARLOCK GAMES by Richard Lee Byers

Mark McIntyre, the newest cadet at Hudson Military Academy, is barely in town a week when he's forced into fighting a jock from Cooper High—Hudson's main competition. At first, Mark wants nothing to do with the rivalry. He's more interested in Laurie Frank, his new girlfriend. But when fellow Hudson cadet Greg Tobias urges him to fight back, Mark suddenly finds himself helping other cadets play violent pranks on Cooper High. What Mark doesn't know is that Greg is a centuries-old warlock who's playing a sick and deadly game with a fellow demon . . . a chess game in which Hudson and Cooper High students are being used as pawns!

AND COMING NEXT MONTH!

#4 THE MASK by Nick Baron

Sheila Holland is an average-looking girl, but she feels like an ugly duckling. Then, while looking for a costume for the Nightmare Club's Halloween party, she finds a weird mask at an antique barn. When she puts it on, she changes into a real knockout. Soon she's getting lots of attention—even sexy Ian Montgomery is pursuing her! But when good-looking kids start dying, Sheila begins to suspect the horrible truth . . . the mask has a deadly guardian. Each time Sheila wears it, he grows stronger. And unless she rejects the mask's amazing magic very soon, the guardian will make her his prisoner forever!

#1: JOY RIDE
Richard Lee Byers

Z·FAVE
KENSINGTON PUBLISHING CORP.

Z-FAVE BOOKS are published by

Kensington Publishing Corp.
475 Park Avenue South
New York, NY 10016

The Nightmare Club series created and edited by Alice
Alfonsi.

First Printing: August, 1993

Printed in the United States of America

For Ken, Denise, and Colleen Claire

One

The old red Mustang drifted to the right, and suddenly its front tire was bumping on the dirt at the side of the narrow road. "Be careful!" Karen warned.

Mike jerked the steering wheel. Rubber screeched, and the car swerved back into its lane. He turned his head to frown at the girl sitting in the bucket seat beside his. "You sure are uptight tonight," he said.

This time Karen was almost certain she smelled beer on his breath, beneath the mediciny scent of some kind of mouthwash. She wondered again if she ought to ask him about it. The road didn't have any streetlights. It twisted constantly, and trees pressed close on either side. If he lost control for an instant, the car could crash into one.

But lots of kids sneaked a beer occasionally. Probably they shouldn't, but they did. She didn't know that Mike was *drunk,* and she didn't want to make him mad and spoil their first real date. She'd known and liked him all her life, even at the age when girls thought boys were gross and vice versa, and now, with his wavy brown hair, brown eyes, and tall, rangy build, he'd grown into one of the cutest guys at Cooper High. "I'm sorry," she said. "I just think you're driving a little fast."

He scowled, but he eased up a little on the gas. The speedometer needle swung to the left. "You want to go slow; we'll go slow," he said sullenly.

Karen tried to relax, but her fingers still fidgeted with the ends of her shoulder-length red hair. "I wonder what this Night Owl Club is like," she said, trying to get the conversation started again.

"Probably boring, like everything else in Cooper Hollow. I wish we lived closer to New York. *That's* where the action is."

"I hope you're wrong about the club, because you're right about the town. It could use something to liven it up. Maybe the club will be all right. They advertised that it's got dancing and games. Live music on the weekends."

Mike grinned at her. "Well, I'm sure it'll have a real party atmosphere, considering that the building's about a million years old and hundreds of kids *died* there." The Mustang's engine growled a little louder. The speedometer needle crept to the right again.

She considered mentioning it, then decided not to. "You believe that story? About the orphans and the fire?"

"Sure. I believe the place is haunted, too."

She snorted. "Yeah, right."

"I do." He lowered his voice, trying to sound spooky. "A few years ago, Bill, Pete, and I camped out overnight in these woods. A storm came up, and we heard the orphans screaming, just like people say you can when it rains."

"You are so *full* of it."

He raised an eyebrow. "Don't mock what you can't understand, foolish mortal." He was trying even harder to sound like Creature Feature now. "Before this night has passed, we ourselves may behold the living dead." Karen felt the car begin to drift again.

Her head snapped around, so she could look out the windshield. The Mustang was left of the center line, and a few feet ahead, the road bent to the *right*.

10

They were only seconds away from crashing into a stand of pines. And Mike didn't know it! He was watching her, not the road.

"Look out!" she screamed.

Mike turned his head, then gasped. He stamped on the brake and wrenched the wheel. Its brakes squealing, the car began to spin.

Beyond the windows, the world whirled. The plastic dinosaur hanging from the rearview mirror lashed about at the end of its cord. Karen's body tensed. She was too scared to scream.

The car bounced as it left the road, and for a second, she was sure it was going to flip over. Instead it slid sideways toward a pine, and now she was certain the tree trunk would come smashing through her door. But the Mustang stopped moving mere inches before hitting it. Needled branches had bent and squashed against her window.

For a moment, she felt numb and dazed. She wondered why everything seemed so quiet until she realized that the engine had stalled. Then a wave of terror washed through her, and she was suddenly desperate to escape the car.

"Get out!" she shrieked.

"What?" Mike said stupidly. His face was white as paper.

"Get out!" She shoved at him. "I want out of the car!"

"All right!" He got out. She squirmed awkwardly past the gearshift, then scrambled out behind him. She turned her back on the Mustang and him and stood trembling, hugging herself.

After a while, she heard him step up behind her. "Are you all right?" he asked.

She drew a deep breath, trying to calm down. "I think so. Are you?"

"Yeah. And so's the car. We're lucky."

11

Luckier than you deserve, she thought angrily. But they *were* okay, and it *had* been an accident, and he *was* her friend, so she guessed there was no point in screaming at him. "Yeah."

"Well. Do you want to go on and check out the club?"

"I suppose." She turned to face him. "But I'm driving."

He blinked at her. "My mom told me not to let anyone else drive my car. Look, I'm sorry I scared you, but anybody can have an accident. I'll be more careful, honest."

"You can't drive," she said. "You're drunk."

For an instant, he looked surprised. Confused. Maybe even guilty. Then he sneered. "No way."

"You are. I can smell beer on you. How many did you have?"

He frowned. "I don't know. Maybe one or two."

"If you *admit* to one or two, I bet it's more like a six-pack!" When she heard how nasty she sounded, she winced. She liked him. She wanted to reason with him, not make him angry. But being terrified had made *her* so angry that suddenly she couldn't hold it in.

"You're calling me a liar," he said. "Nice. Look, it doesn't matter how many I had. The important thing is, I can handle it."

"Oh, obviously." She waved her hand at the Mustang.

"I told you: *anybody* can have an accident. I kept us from hitting anything, didn't I?"

She sighed. "Please, Mike, I don't want to fight. C'mon, we're friends. Can't you just humor me? Let me drive so we can stop arguing and get on with our date. What difference does it make anyway?"

He shook his head. "My mom would kill me."

"Then I'm walking home. Good night."

"Don't be dumb. You don't want to be alone in these woods." He started talking in his Creature Feature voice. "E-vil spirits stalk them."

"You are *so* immature!" Tossing her head, she turned and strode back down the road. Even as upset as she was, she couldn't help noticing that the ranks of trees *did* look creepy in the chilly darkness. But she didn't believe in ghosts, and even if there were any, she doubted they'd be as dangerous as climbing back into the Mustang with Mike.

Two

Mike watched Karen until she disappeared into the night. He wanted to go after her, but he didn't know what to say.

He wondered what to do with the rest of the evening. He supposed he could check out the new club by himself. Sighing, he climbed back into the Mustang.

When he turned the key in the ignition, the starter made a tired, wheezing sound. He realized that when he'd gotten out of the stalled car, he'd left the lights on. And his battery was old and weak. He hoped that he wouldn't wind up hiking home himself.

But to his relief, the next time he twisted the key, his engine roared to life. Immediately, he felt a little better. Driving almost always made him feel better. Free. A beer or two always mellowed him out, and then he was king of the world.

He eased the car back onto the road, then drove on through the woods. After a minute, the club came into view.

To Mike, the big brick building still looked like an orphanage, one run by greedy caretakers, who embezzled the children's food money, starved them, and beat them if they complained. He could almost see sad, hollow-cheeked little faces peering from the shuttered second-story windows. Crooked, leafless trees pressed close around the structure, as if they were whispering secrets. There were no lights in the small parking lot, and only one, a blue one, over the front door. There was no sign. If he hadn't heard rap music faintly pulsing through the walls, he might have thought the club hadn't opened as scheduled.

"Night Owl Club," he said sourly. "Looks more like a Night*mare* Club to me."

Wishing that he weren't alone, and that he had another beer, he climbed out of the car. Someone giggled.

Startled, he spun around. At first, he didn't see anything. Then a soft voice murmured, "Over here."

He pivoted. A blur of gray light hung in the darkness. He blinked his eyes, then rubbed them. The newcomer chuckled. When he looked again, the smudge of glimmer had sharpened into focus. In fact, he had the funny feeling that he could see *too* well, as if the newcomer's body really was glowing.

The stranger was a beautiful girl, small and slim, with fair skin, big, dark eyes, and brown hair. She was wearing a silky red dress. She *looked* his age, but somehow she *felt* older. Sophisticated. More mature. That thought reminded him of Karen's parting putdown, and he frowned. His expression must have amused the newcomer, because she laughed again.

"Such a face," she said. "Boys are usually glad to see me."

"Sorry," he said. "It's just that you startled me. Where did you come from?"

"Out of the night," she answered lightly. She moved closer, and he noticed a tiny scar on her forehead, just below the hairline. She smelled of some flowery perfume. Underneath that scent lay a faint tang of alcohol. When he caught it, he wished again for another beer. She offered her hand. "Joyce Carrier. But

15

everyone calls me Joy. You can, too."

"Mike Davis." Her grip was firm, but her skin was soft. He released her hand a little reluctantly. "I'm a junior at Cooper High. Do you go there?"

"Are you alone?" she asked, ignoring his question.

He sighed. "I am now."

"Then this is our first date. Unless you'd rather be by yourself to sulk."

"N—no!" he stammered, pleased but caught off guard. "I'd like company."

She took his arm. "Then let's go in."

When they passed through the door, Mike was surprised. He'd expected the inside of the club to be as ancient-looking and uninviting as the outside. It wasn't. Much of the ground floor had been converted into a combination dance club, game room, and snack bar. There were booths lit by candles in colored glass bowls, with red leather cushions on the seats. A jukebox, the source of the music, stood against the wall, while a faceted silver ball hung above a spacious dance floor. In the rear was a bar with a brass foot rail; behind it, the soda machines and kitchen. An arched doorway led to video games and pool, air hockey, and fooz ball tables. All in all, the place looked like it might actually be fun.

Even though it was Tuesday and a school night, some other kids had turned out to look over the club. Mike knew some of the kids were from Cooper High. There were others he didn't recognize. Some of the guys wore the gray-with-navy-blue-trim toy-soldier uniforms of Hudson Military Academy. He guessed the unfamiliar girls were probably students at Cooper Riding Academy, the other snotty boarding school in the area. It occurred to him that, as flashy as Joy was dressed, she might go there, too.

His friends didn't notice him, and he didn't call out to them. Joy didn't greet anyone either, just led him

16

to a booth.

As they sat down, a new, louder rap song started playing. She made a face at the jukebox. "You don't like rap?" he asked.

"It's horrible," she answered.

"I like alternative better myself," he said. "Do you live in the Hollow? Why haven't I seen you before?"

"I was away for a long time. In fact, I just got back."

He opened his mouth to ask where she'd be going to school. "Would you like a menu?" a cold voice inquired.

Mike jerked around. A tall, thin man was standing beside the booth. With his shock of snow-white hair, his high forehead, and his curved nose, like a hawk's beak or a sword blade, he looked like a mad scientist. But judging from his apron and the pad and pencil in his hands, Mike figured he must work there. Probably he was Jake Demos, the owner, whose name had been on the advertising flyer. "I don't know," Mike said, looking toward Joy. "I'm not hungry, but—"

"I'm not either," she said. "I just want a ginger ale."

He looked up at the waiter. "Then we only need a ginger ale and a Coke."

The old man squinted at him for a moment, looking puzzled, then said, "Whatever. You must be thirsty." He turned and walked away.

"That guy's weird," said Mike.

Joy grinned.

"What's so funny?"

"Nothing," she said. "It's just that suddenly, I feel very *safe*."

"Come again?"

"I mean, I feel happy, being with you. I just wish you felt the same. Why don't you tell me what happened?"

"If this really is a date, it would be pretty stupid for

17

me to talk about another girl."

"But we won't be able to have any fun until you brighten up, and I think you need to talk to do that." She laid her hand on top of his. "Please. I really want to hear."

He shrugged. "Well . . . okay. I was supposed to come here with this girl Karen Bradley. I've known her forever and I like her pretty well." He pictured Karen's turned-up nose, freckles, and bright green eyes, and winced. It hurt to know that she was disgusted with him. On the other hand, he resented being made to feel the pain. He explained what had happened on the road.

When he finished, Joy said, "This Karen must be dumb or hysterical or something. It's obvious you aren't drunk. You aren't staggering or talking funny."

He nodded. "That's right."

"She probably doesn't drink, does she?"

"I don't think so."

Joy smiled. "A goody-two-shoes. She doesn't know how to have fun, so she tries to make sure nobody else has any, either. You're lucky to be rid of her."

He blinked, feeling confused. On one hand, he liked hearing Joy say that he'd been right and Karen had been wrong. But it bothered him that she was slamming Karen, and taking it for granted that the two of them wouldn't be friends anymore. He was still trying to decide how to answer when Mr. Demos came back to the booth, a tray with two sodas in his hands.

To Mike's surprise, the old man set both drinks in front of him. "A Coke and a ginger ale," he said. "Will there be anything else?"

Joy shook her head. "No," Mike said.

Mr. Demos squinted at him for a moment, then turned, and walked away.

Now that the old man was gone, and it was too late

to say anything, Mike started to get mad. "That guy's a terrible waiter," he said. "Rude. He never looked at you or spoke to you once, and he put your drink in front of me."

"Oh, well. Old people get funny. Sometimes they take a dislike to somebody for no reason at all. Don't worry about it."

"I'm not, but I won't leave him a tip, either."

She laughed. "My hero." She picked up the ginger ale. "Drink some of your drink."

He sipped the Coke, then set it back down. Joy opened her black leather purse, rummaged inside it, then brought out a gleaming silver flask.

Mike looked around frantically. Fortunately, Mr. Demos wasn't in sight. But he could come back at any time. "Are you crazy? Put that away before the old man sees it!"

She giggled. "Don't you want another drink?"

He hesitated. He did, and he'd always been curious what hard liquor was like. Up till now, he'd only tried beer and wine. "I guess, but—"

"Then relax. I promise, no one will see." She unscrewed the cap of the flask. A sharp odor, the same one he'd smelled beneath her perfume, filled the air. She poured clear liquid into each glass, then put the metal bottle away again. She raised the ginger ale. "Cheers."

After a moment, he realized she wanted him to tap his glass against hers. He did, then took a cautious sip of the spiked Coke.

The liquor's flavor reminded him of pine needles. Together, it and the cola tasted nasty, and the drink burned going down his throat. For a second, he was afraid he was going to gag.

"What is that stuff?" he gasped.

Joy grinned. "Just good old bathtub gin."

"*Bathtub* gin?"

19

"It's just an expression. Do you like it?"

He opened his mouth to tell her he hadn't liked it at all. Then a warm glow bloomed in his stomach. A wave of pleasure, more powerful than any drink had ever given him before, swept through his body. He realized he was grinning like an idiot. "I guess," he said.

She smirked. "I thought you would." She took out the flask again, and added more liquor to the Coke. He took another sip. This time, the mixture tasted better.

"Drink up," Joy said. "Then you can take me for a drive."

Three

Pearl Jam's "Jeremy" blared out of the clock radio, jolting Mike awake. He realized instantly that he felt sicker than he ever had before. His head pounded in time with the beat of the song, and the sunlight streaming through the curtains burned his squinting eyes. His stomach was upset.

He fumbled at the clock, finally managing to switch the music off. He noticed that he was still dressed and lying on top of the blanket on his bed. It looked like he'd been a little wasted by the time he got home.

After he and Joy had left the Night Owl Club, they'd spent hours driving around, talking, laughing, and drinking. First they'd mixed gin with sodas they'd bought at a carryout, and later, they took nips straight from the flask. He couldn't remember much of what they'd said to one another, but he knew they'd had a really good time.

Abruptly he realized that, even if Joy had told him where she lived or went to school or her phone number, he'd forgotten. He couldn't even remember where he'd dropped her off.

Oh, well, the Hollow and its surrounding small towns were tiny enough that he was sure he could find her. But if there were holes in his memory, maybe Karen had a point. Maybe he was drinking a little too much.

He decided he'd take it a little easier—at least when he was drinking liquor—until he got used to it, anyway. He lurched up off the bed and shuffled down the hall to the bathroom. The door to his mom's room was still shut. No breakfast again today unless he fixed it himself, not that his stomach felt in any shape for eating.

His mom had been going downhill for the last three years, beginning when his dad left them. Mike sometimes thought that, in time, she might have gotten over it, but then she hurt her back on the job. Once the disability payments started and she no longer had to go out and work, it was like she'd decided not to do *anything,* including pay attention to her kid. Most days she just lay around, sleeping and watching TV.

He hated seeing her like that. Hated it so much that sometimes he felt like he'd fall apart himself if it weren't for basketball. Not only did he love to play, but thanks to the sport, he knew his life was going someplace. Because he had talent. Last year, only Pete Perry had scored higher. Their team was so strong they'd made it to the State finals.

The college scouts were already drooling over Pete, and according to Coach Yarborough, Mike had what it took to win a scholarship, too. So he knew he'd be going to a good school, and then maybe even to the pros. Who knew, he might be the next Patrick Ewing!

He just wished his mom would show more interest when he talked about his plans. It was hard to stay excited about even a bright future when the person who was supposed to be his biggest backer didn't seem to care.

He wondered if he could convince her to visit his Aunt Linda in New York later this fall. Maybe she could do some shopping, and that would cheer her up. And he could catch a Knicks game with his cousin Del, just like he used to with his dad. Maybe

Karen could come—

Well, no, she couldn't. Wouldn't. Not anymore. Joy was his girlfriend now.

Much as he liked her, he still regretted that things hadn't worked out with Karen. Part of him wished they could make up.

Sighing, he trudged on into the john. His hangover seemed to worsen with every step. A cottony thickness in his skull made it hard to think. He wondered if he should stay home sick from school, then realized he couldn't. Basketball tryouts were today. He'd just have to hope he'd start feeling better as the day went on.

Cleaning up helped a little. At least showering took the greasy, sweaty feeling off his skin, and brushing his teeth removed most of the nasty taste from his mouth. Maybe he'd at least make it through homeroom without dying or throwing up.

When he was dressed, he grabbed the blue nylon backpack in which he carried his books, then went downstairs. He saw the remains of a take-out Chinese meal on the floor. Darn it, he and Mom lived in a nice house. It would *look* nice if they could only work together to keep it up. If only there were some way to get her to *care* about things again. To turn her back into the person she used to be.

Maybe they could go out to eat tonight. It might do her good just to get out of this crummy house.

Stepping outside into the crisp autumn air, he saw that the rust-spotted Mustang was parked in the driveway at an angle, its front bumper only inches away from the back of his mom's Corolla. For some reason, he hadn't pulled on into the garage. Maybe he hadn't been able to maneuver well enough.

Resolving again to go a little easier on the hard stuff, he tossed his pack into the Mustang's backseat, then climbed in. He twisted the key in the ignition,

23

and the starter moaned sluggishly.

"Come on," he said, "it's not that cold." The car *had* to start. He'd already missed the school bus.

"Having trouble?" a girl's voice asked.

He whirled. Joy was sitting in the bucket seat next to him, grinning. His heart hammered, and he realized he wasn't only startled because she'd appeared out of nowhere. For some reason, he hadn't expected to see her *in the daylight*.

"Where did you come from?" he asked.

"Didn't your parents tell you about the birds and the bees?"

He frowned. "I mean . . . you were just there, suddenly."

"I said hello, then got in. You told me you'd give me a ride to school, remember?"

He didn't, but there was no point in saying so. Then he *would* look stupid, or like he was trying to brush her off. "Right," he mumbled. He noticed she was wearing the same shiny red dress she'd had on last night. She'd seemed overdressed at the Night Owl Club; at school in that outfit she'd look even more out of place. But he guessed she could wear what she wanted. Maybe she was making a fashion statement like those girls who shopped at thrift stores. What was *really* strange was that the outfit looked clean and fresh, not wrinkled at all. Maybe she had two just alike.

"You're staring at me," she said. "Is it because I'm so gorgeous, you can't tear your eyes away?"

He snorted. "You like yourself, don't you?" A car parked on the street honked its horn. The noise jabbed pain into his forehead, and he winced.

"You look terrible." She put her hand on his shoulder. "Are you sick?"

"A little hung over," he admitted.

"No problem." She opened the black leather bag

24

and took out the flask. "You just need the hair of the dog that bit you. A shot kills a hangover, didn't you know that?"

He suddenly realized he wanted a drink. In fact, he was surprised at how much. But alcohol was for evenings, not mornings. For partying, not when you had business to take care of. "No, I'd better not."

"Oh, come on. I had a nip already, and I seem all right, don't I? Heck, at the moment, I'm doing a lot better than you."

She did look fine, not sick at all. "I don't know. It seems like a bad habit to get into." He turned the key again. The starter wheezed without catching. The car horn blared once more. Mike gritted his teeth against another throb of pain.

"Who's talking about making it a habit?" Joy said. "I'm just saying: have one drink this one time, so you won't feel like crap and can do what you're supposed to do."

He guessed one sip couldn't hurt. And if Joy said it would make him feel better, it was worth a try. He took the flask, unscrewed the cap, and swigged.

When he did, he realized that some time during the night, the pine-needle taste and the burning sensation had come to seem pleasant. The gin hit his stomach, and a tide of warmth washed through him. It soothed his stomach, eased the pain in his forehead, and dissolved the muddiness in his brain. The sensation was so pleasant that he took two more swallows without thinking about it. Then he handed the silver bottle back to her, feeling a little reluctant to let it go.

Joy grinned. "Feel better, don't you?" Nodding, he twisted the ignition key. The engine started. "Then let's ride!"

Four

Karen stowed her books and clarinet case in her locker, grabbed her lunch, clanged the gray metal door shut, and snapped the padlock closed. The corridor around her was full of rushing, jabbering kids, all eager to eat and talk with their friends.

She was talking too, about last night. But now she was beginning to regret it. Maybe it was wrong to discuss Mike behind his back. She was worried about him, though. Maybe she wanted somebody to tell her that there wasn't any reason to be.

Unfortunately, Joan Adams wasn't doing that as she peered down at Karen. Joan was the tallest girl in the junior class, and she had to look down at just about everybody. "You did the right thing," she said. "If you'd gotten back in that car, he could have killed you. He'll probably kill himself, or get arrested for drunk driving, before the end of the year."

Karen frowned in irritation. "You sound like you're wishing it on him."

Joan tossed her head. Her frosted curls and the big gold hoops in her ears flew about. "I am not," she said, "and you know it. I'm just stating facts. And evaluating the data." Joan was a math and science whiz and a computer nerd, and the word "data" seemed to turn up in every other sentence out of her mouth.

"All right," Karen said. "I'm sorry. But just because he drank and drove once—"

"You know Pete and Mike hang out together." Karen nodded. Pete Perry was a senior and Cooper High's best basketball player. He was also Joan's boyfriend. She was lucky he liked her; he was one of the few guys in school taller than she was. "Well, he says that Mike can really put beer away."

Karen snorted. "If Pete saw that, then he was drinking, too. Why aren't we worrying about *him?*"

"Because he doesn't drink and get behind the wheel."

"He doesn't have a car."

"And because his father wasn't an alcoholic."

They started walking toward the cafeteria, past classroom doors, water fountains, and a display case full of paintings kids had done in art class. "You can't condemn him for what his dad was," Karen said. "That isn't fair at all."

"I'm not *judging* him," Joan replied. "But drinking problems can be inherited. The data proves it." The tall girl thought she knew everything there was to know about the human mind. Maybe because her dad was a psychiatrist. Actually, Joan thought she knew everything about most other subjects, too.

"If he is in danger of becoming an alcoholic, somebody should help him before things get bad—before he has a wreck," Karen stated.

"You can't," Joan said. "Before you can help an alcoholic, he has to admit he has a problem, and they don't do that until something awful happens. It's called hitting bottom."

Karen shook her head. "I don't buy that. I mean, first of all, I'm not convinced that Mike could become an alcoholic. And even if he could, I don't believe that he has to ruin his whole life before he can face the problem. Maybe that's true of most drinkers,

27

but it doesn't have to be that way for him. People are different."

Ahead, voices murmured and dishes clinked; the girls had almost reached the cafeteria. "I'm warning you," Joan said. "If you get involved in his problems, they'll be your problems, too. You ought to go out with Dave Francis. He likes you." Two sophomore boys pushed by. One said something about "the Giraffe," Joan's hated nickname, and she scowled.

"I didn't say I was going to try to solve Mike's problems," Karen said. "But I'm not ready to stop being his friend, either. If he doesn't mind, I'm going to eat lunch with him, just like we've been doing." She hesitated. "You know that usually, you'd be welcome to sit with us. But today—"

"You have to patch things up," Joan said. "Don't worry, I understand. But remember what I told you."

They stepped through the cafeteria door. The cafeteria was a big room filled with rows of long tables. The line of kids who didn't brown-bag their lunches ran from the entrance along the wall to the serving area in the back. Signs read, PLEASE THROW AWAY YOUR TRASH, and PLEASE RETURN TRAYS TO THE WINDOW. A scarlet and white banner with the words COOPER HIGH, HOME OF THE RED DEVILS and a picture of an imp on it hung from the ceiling. Mr. Cummings, the bald, chunky chemistry teacher, stood beside a window with his arms folded, glaring as if he expected the kids to riot like convicts in a prison movie.

Joan got in line. Karen looked around the room. After a moment, she spotted Mike. He'd already gotten a tray and sat down at a table. Though the gray metal folding chairs were filling up, there was an empty seat beside him. Maybe he'd saved it for her. Smiling, she bought a Diet Seven-Up from the soda machine, then walked toward him.

As she approached, she heard whispers and snickering. Of course, during lunch, the cafeteria always buzzed with voices and laughter. But this time, some instinct warned Karen that the sounds had something to do with *her*.

She turned in time to see several kids lowering their eyes. She glanced down at herself. Her jeans were zipped. There was no toilet paper stuck to her shoe. As far as she could tell without a mirror, she looked okay. There was no reason for anyone to make fun of her.

Well, people gossiped and giggled about all kinds of stupid things. She decided to ignore them. She walked on. When she reached the table, she pulled out the chair, sat down, and said, "Hi."

Mike jerked around, looking startled and confused. If she'd surprised him, maybe he hadn't wanted her to sit with him after all. She felt a little disappointed. "Uh, hi," he said. "Somebody was sitting there." He sat up straight and peered around. "But, I don't know, I guess she left."

A boy across the table chuckled.

Karen said, "Well, I'm glad she did, because I want to talk to you." She lowered her voice, even though she knew that anyone who really wanted to listen would be able to hear her anyway. "About last night. Are you mad at me?"

"No" he said. "Are you mad at me?"

"Not anymore. In fact, maybe we could try another date. If you want to."

He squirmed. "Well. You know I like you. But, after you split, something happened. I met somebody at the Night Owl Club."

Someone behind Karen whispered. She couldn't catch the words, but the voice had a nasty tone. Someone else laughed in response. Now she guessed she understood what all the hilarity was about.

29

People had known that Mike was going to dump her, and they thought it was funny.

Well, she wouldn't give them the satisfaction of seeing that she was hurt, even though the rejection stung more than she could have expected. She opened the soda can and removed a turkey sandwich and apple from her brown bag; maneuvers that gave her a few seconds to pull herself together. When she spoke, her voice was steady. "You're a fast worker."

He squirmed again. "It wasn't like that. It just happened."

I hate this, she thought. I ought to get up and walk away. But she'd known Mike forever. If she couldn't date him, she guessed she'd rather keep his friendship than not talk to him at all. She smiled. "Hey, it's okay. It's not like we had some hot and heavy romance going. Our whole dating career lasted what, about half an hour?"

He smiled back. She could see he was grateful that she wasn't going to give him a hard time. "About that, I guess."

"So who is she?"

"Her name is Joyce Carrier. But people call her Joy. She just moved back to the Hollow."

"From where?"

Mike shook his head. "I'm not sure."

"Where's she go to school?"

"Here. That's who was sitting with me before you came."

And I'll bet you were drooling all over her, Karen thought. That's how all these jerks knew you didn't like *me* anymore. She couldn't help feeling jealous.

But she wasn't just jealous, she was puzzled. Cooper Hollow wasn't a huge town, and Cooper High wasn't a huge school. When a new kid transferred in, usually everyone knew it right away. So how come she hadn't noticed the wonderful Joy? "Is she a junior?" she asked.

Mike shrugged. "I guess."

She tilted her head. "Don't you *know?*"

"No," he said. "What's the difference? What is this, the third degree?"

"No," she said, suddenly feeling a little ashamed. She'd promised herself she wouldn't show she was upset, but her anger was leaking out as usual. Her dad said she had a redhead's temper, and she guessed it was true. "It just seems funny you didn't find out a little more about her. But it doesn't matter, and I'm sorry for being nosy." She offered her hand. "We're still friends, right?"

They shook. "Sure," Mike said.

"And you won't drink and drive anymore, right?"

He frowned. "All right! Whatever! I just don't want to hear about it anymore! I think I should go find Joy. See you." Though he'd eaten only half his burger, and had plenty of fries left, he jumped up and carried his tray away.

Startled by his sudden anger, Karen simply sat and watched him vanish through the door. Realizing she was too upset to eat, she took one sip of soda, and carried her lunch to one of the green plastic garbage cans. Then she left the cafeteria herself.

Out in the hall, three girls who'd been sitting near her stood murmuring and giggling together. One was Anne Morgan, a black girl with plaited hair. Like Karen, she played first clarinet in band and orchestra. She shot a sneaky glance in Karen's direction.

Karen's temper snapped. She stalked up to the three girls. "What's the big joke?" she demanded. "So Mike broke up with me for a new girl! So what? I remember when Howard Scott dumped you, Anne. I didn't make fun of you!"

The three girls honestly looked shocked. "Nobody was laughing at *you,* Karen," Anne replied. "Really.

We were laughing at *Mike,* and wondering if you felt weird, talking to him."

"I don't understand," Karen said. "Why would you laugh at him?"

"His wonderful new girlfriend," Anne said. "The one he was introducing around. The one who was supposedly sitting in your seat before you got there." Her two companions snickered.

"What about her?" Karen asked impatiently.

"Nobody was there. Mike was talking to an empty chair. At first everybody thought he was kidding around, but then we realized he's gone nuts."

Five

Mike dribbled, and the basketball thumped the polished floor. He felt frustrated. Clumsy and confused. The Shirts, the opposing team, were all over him, and as far as he could see, his fellow Skins could have been on some other court playing a different game.

Well, he had to do something, or the Shirts were going to steal the ball. Spinning, he jumped into the air and shot. The ball missed not only the basket but the backboard. It bounced off the yellow-painted cinderblock wall.

Coach Yarborough blew a shrill blast on his whistle. "Okay, that's it for today," he said. "Hit the showers. Same time tomorrow. And then I want to see some hustle! Especially from you, Davis! Were you asleep out there, or what?"

The Skins shuffled over to the bleachers to pick up their T-shirts. Dave Francis poked Mike in the arm. "Why wouldn't you pass to me?" he demanded. "Half the time I was wide open." Dave played sports more *seriously* than any other guy Mike knew. He couldn't stand for his team to look bad for a single second, even when they weren't playing a real game, just showing Coach what they could do.

"You were not!" Mike said.

"Man, you have really lost it," Dave said, sneering. He walked away.

Mike followed him and the other guys down the concrete stairs into the locker room. He didn't feel like talking to any of the rest of them, so he lagged behind. By the time he reached the bottom of the steps, the showers had already begun to hiss.

But even so, he hadn't managed to avoid everyone. Pete Perry was sitting on the bench in front of his locker, untying his high-tops. "Are you okay?" he asked.

Mike tried to open the padlock on the locker door. His fingers shook, and he dialed past the first number in the combination. "Yes," he said, annoyed. "I just had this conversation. I don't need to have it again."

Pete ran his long fingers through his sweaty blond hair. "I don't mean to hassle you," he said. "I just want to help if you need it. You didn't look so great today. I mean, sure, you'll make the team, but if you don't do better tomorrow, Coach might not let you start. And you need games to get your scoring stats up. That's what the college scouts look at."

Mike pulled down on the lock. He *thought* he'd dialed the combination right the second time, but the mechanism didn't pop open. Suddenly angry, he punched the locker door. The crash echoed through the room.

Pete stared at him. "Hey," he said, then lowered his voice. "Have you been drinking?"

"No!" Mike said. And he hadn't, not really. Just a few tiny sips from Joy's flask, when they'd met between classes. Not enough to matter.

"Sure," Pete said doubtfully. "Okay. I was just thinking that if you *have* been—"

"Look," Mike said, "if you want to help me, give me a break on the court." Pete had played for the

34

Shirts. "You were on top of me every second. What were you trying to prove?"

Pete shrugged. "This is my senior year. I have to play well. I've got a scholarship riding on it. You know that."

Yeah, right, Mike thought bitterly. Like the Hollow's answer to Michael Jordan needed to prove himself in a tryout game. "If you can't see your way clear to *really* help me, then just leave me alone, okay?"

Pete scowled. The expression looked out of place on a face that almost always smiled. "Hey, whatever you want." He rose and walked away, the untied laces of his sneakers dragging on the concrete floor.

For a moment, Mike wanted to call him back. After all, Pete was supposed to be his buddy. But a real friend wouldn't all but call him a liar.

He decided to skip a shower. What the heck, it was the end of the day, so who cared if his armpits stank? He just wanted to avoid another irritating conversation like the two he'd just had. When he finally managed to fumble open his padlock, he dressed quickly, then left.

By now, the school's halls were empty. His footsteps echoed. Outside the building, things were just as quiet. The kids and the line of yellow buses had gone. There were only a few cars left in the student parking lot, his Mustang among them.

When he was halfway to the car, Joy opened the door, climbed out, and waved at him.

He stopped, confused. He'd been looking straight at the Mustang's windshield, and he could have sworn there hadn't been anyone inside. For a moment, he felt scared. A chill seemed to ooze across his skin.

Then he frowned, annoyed with himself for being so jumpy. Obviously, she *had* been in the car. Either a reflection on the glass had kept him from seeing her, or she'd been messing with something on the floor.

35

What other explanation could there be? He hurried on.

She hugged him as if they'd dated for months instead of only once. He tried to recall whether she'd hugged him like that last night. He frowned when he realized that again he couldn't remember. "I thought you'd walk home, or take the bus," he said. "I told you I had basketball tryouts, didn't I?"

"Yes," she said, "but I decided I'd rather wait on you than go another way. Maybe I shouldn't have. You don't look very happy to see me."

"Believe me, I am," he said. "It's just that except for the few minutes I spent with you, it hasn't been that great a day."

"Well, let's start making it better," she said. She opened her bag.

He knew she was getting the gin. As usual, she didn't seem at all worried that some adult might see them, that they could get in trouble. He looked around. Joy's luck was holding. Except for the two of them, the lined asphalt lot was still deserted.

She brought out the silver flask. It shone in the late afternoon sunlight. Like before, Mike was a little surprised at how much he wanted a drink.

Still, for a second, he wondered if he *should* start in on it again. Maybe it *had* messed up his ball-playing. And he didn't want to wake up with another hangover.

But he didn't have to play ball again until tomorrow afternoon. There was no reason he couldn't party now and be in fine shape again by then. And if he just drank a little less, he'd avoid the hangover. He glanced around again, then uncapped the flask and took a swig.

A sweet warmth tingled through his body. He smiled.

"I told you I'd make it better," Joy said. "Let's get

out of here." They climbed into the Mustang. For a change, it started on the first try. "Now tell me what went wrong."

He drove toward the parking lot exit. Feeling the car respond to the movements of his hands and feet relaxed him even more. He took another drink, then handed the flask back to her. "We're always talking about me. Tell me about you. How did you like your first day at Cooper? What classes are you taking?"

"Cooper's boring, except for you," she said, sipping from the flask. "And my classes are the dullest part of it, so I don't want to think about them now. Tell me what's the matter. That's what friends are for."

"Well, okay," he said. "If you really want to hear." He turned the Mustang onto the street. His hand slipped off the steering wheel, and the car swerved left of the center line. He hastily grabbed the wheel and brought the vehicle back under control. "First off, all day I've had this weird feeling that people are laughing at me behind my back. Then, at tryouts, I didn't do that good. And afterward, Dave and Pete got on my case about it."

"That's always depressing," she said, "when you find out that people you thought were friends, really aren't. But it's not quite so bad if you have a *real* friend, somebody who's truly on your side."

He smiled. "You mean, like you."

"Sure," she said. "You know, if people have stopped being nice to you, it's probably because you don't fit in with them anymore. I've noticed you're a lot more grownup than anyone else at school."

He shrugged, flattered but doubtful that it was true. "I don't know about that."

"I do. Think about it: you do the things adults do." She passed him the flask. He took a drink. "If you didn't play well today, I bet it's because you aren't really interested in kids' games anymore. You just haven't realized it yet."

He shook his head, feeling confused. "You're right, sometimes I do feel different than Pete and Karen and the others. Once in a while, I even think I'd like to go away without telling anybody." Like his father had, he thought with a pang of guilt. "Down to New York City. Get a job and an apartment and a whole new life. But other times, I like it here. And I do like basketball."

Joy shrugged. "I suppose it's all right. But I'm going to teach you some more exciting games. What do you say we go for a drive."

Six

On weekday nights, there weren't many people driving in town. Mike was glad to have the streets to himself. For some reason, there'd been a lot of jerks on the road this evening. Cars kept suddenly appearing just a few feet ahead of him—obviously, they were pulling onto the highway without looking to see if anyone was coming. To avoid rear-ending them, he either had to hit his brakes or swerve around them. Usually, it seemed like less trouble, or at least less aggravation, to swerve.

Joy twisted the radio tuner dial, cutting off the Black Crows' "She Talks to Angels." Old-fashioned music, a mix of brass and woodwinds, came out of the speakers.

Mike shook his head. They'd been jokingly arguing over the radio all night. "Don't you like *any* modern music?" he asked.

"No," Joy said. "It's just noise. Jazz is a million times better. And that's King Oliver, one of the best jazz men. So listen with respect."

"Well, you sure know a lot about it," said Mike. "Are your parents into this stuff?" He remembered that he still didn't know anything about her family, or even where she lived. For a second, it made him feel funny.

39

She laughed. "No. My parents did—don't like much that I like."

"Oh." He was going to ask more about them, but she handed him the flask. So he took a drink instead.

They rolled by the First Federal Bank with its digital clock. He was startled to see that it was already after ten. "Are you sure you don't want to *do* something?" he asked.

"We are doing something," she said, taking the bottle back. "And I'm having a great time. Aren't you?"

"Yeah," he said. "But I'm worried that you're going to get bored with me, if all we ever do is cruise."

"I love riding around more than just about anything," she said, then sipped from the flask.

The traffic light ahead of them switched from green to yellow. It looked like they could make it past before it turned red, so Mike floored the gas. The Mustang shot forward.

He'd guessed wrong. The light turned red when they were still a few yards in front of it. He stepped on the brake.

As the car began to slow, tires squealing, he realized he'd made a second mistake. He'd been going too fast to stop short of the intersection now. The Mustang was still going to run the red light, and now that the car was losing speed, it was going to take longer.

Well, he told himself, it'll be all right. Nobody else is running around down here at this hour.

The Mustang skidded out into the crossing. White light blazed through Joy's window, turning her into a shadow. Behind the glare of the headlights, Mike made out the bulk of an eighteen wheeler. The truck driver blew his horn.

He started to swerve but he was too close. He'd never turn in time. If Mike couldn't get out of the way, the truck was going to hit him. He down-shifted and stamped on the gas.

40

The eighteen wheeler rushed forward, filling the side window until it looked like the hugest thing in the world. Though it was about to plow through her door, Joy didn't scream or cringe. It was hard for Mike to be sure with the truck's lights dazzling him, but it looked like she was *smiling*.

The Mustang jerked forward. The rush of speed pressed him back in his seat. The eighteen wheeler shot by just inches from his back bumper.

He pulled into a parking space, then sat there shaking. "Are you all right?" he asked.

Joy started to laugh.

Oh, no, he thought wildly, she's hysterical! Maybe it means she's going into shock! "Tell me you're all right!" he begged.

Finally, after a couple of tries, she brought her laughter under control. "I'm fine," she said, dabbing away tears. "But that was so exciting. And you look so *funny!* Do you need to change your underwear?"

"I admit, I was scared," he said, aggravated. "If you weren't, then you're stupid or crazy."

"I'm sorry," she said. "I shouldn't have made fun of you. Of course I was scared. I guess laughing and making jokes is just my way of handling it. This will calm us down." She drank from the flask, then offered it to him.

For a second, he wondered if he should take it. The way he'd misjudged things a moment ago, maybe he'd had enough. But he was still trembling. His heart was pounding. And the gin would relax him. So he took a swallow, and instantly calmed down.

"Feel better?" Joy asked. He nodded. "Then let's roll."

He hesitated. He didn't want to look like a wimp, but he was a little afraid to take the wheel again right away. "Look, maybe we could go for a walk for a while."

41

"No chance. Having an accident, or a near-accident, is like falling off a horse. You have to get right back on, so you won't start being afraid to ride."

"But . . . I just ran a red light. Maybe I'm . . . tired. Maybe I need to take a break."

"Don't be silly. You didn't run the light. The truck did." She leaned close, and put her hand on his. Her dark eyes gleamed.

"No," he said, "I saw —" Suddenly he felt dizzy, and wasn't sure just *what* he'd seen. Maybe the light hadn't turned red.

"It's that truck driver who shouldn't be on the road," Joy said. "You were in perfect control of your car. That's what saved us."

Suddenly, he realized she was right. He took the car out of neutral and pulled out onto the street.

Seven

An hour later, the fuel gauge needle was dipping toward E. Mike said, "We're low on gas. And I'm broke till my mom gives me more money on Saturday. Well, it's late anyway. I'll take you home—"

"I'm not tired," Joy said. "I'm having too much fun."

"But we have school tomorrow," he said. She laughed, and he felt like a foolish little kid. "Well, I guess we don't have to pack it in yet. But we are going to have to stop cruising." He looked out the windshield at the golden half moon and the bright, twinkling stars. "It's a nice night. Maybe—"

Joy said, "Show me your house."

"What?" he said, startled. He didn't usually invite friends over. He didn't like for them to see his mother. He was ashamed of himself for feeling that way, but he couldn't help it.

"Your house," she repeated. "You keep asking about my home. Well, I'm curious about yours, too."

He frowned. "You still haven't told me where you live."

"I'll take you there soon. But for tonight, you show me your place."

Well, maybe it would be all right. With luck, Mom

43

would already be in bed. "I guess it's okay. If we don't make a lot of noise."

She smiled. "I promise, your mother won't hear a peep out of me." She swigged from the flask, then handed it to him.

A few minutes later, he pulled into his driveway. As he'd hoped, the small frame house was dark. In fact, his mom hadn't even bothered to leave the porch light on for him.

When he and Joy climbed out into the cool night breeze, the world spun, and he had to grab at the car to keep from falling. He guessed that, after sitting so many hours, he'd stood up too fast.

But he had to admit there was more to it than that. He knew he wasn't *very* drunk, because he didn't feel out of control, and Joy kept complimenting him on how well he held his liquor. But obviously, he was a *little* more toasted than he'd meant to be. How had that happened?

After a minute, he figured it out. No breakfast, not much lunch, and then he and Joy had never bothered to stop for supper. Everybody knew that alcohol hit you harder if your stomach was empty. He just needed to remember to eat before he partied, and then he wouldn't have any problems.

Since he probably *looked* bombed, he was even more reluctant to go inside. He was pretty sure his mother wasn't going to see him, but if she did, she wouldn't understand that he was just a *little* buzzed. She'd remember his dad's drinking, and maybe freak.

He turned to suggest again that he and Joy go for a walk. But she wasn't where he'd last seen her. Confused, he looked around until he spied her already on the porch. He wondered how she'd gotten there so quickly. "Come on," she said impatiently.

Somehow he felt as if, by reaching the house before he could stop her, she'd grabbed control of the situation. Now he *had* to take her inside. Or maybe he just didn't want to explain why he shouldn't. If he made it sound like he was scared of his mom, Joy would think he was a wimp. "Okay," he said, starting forward. "But remember, we need to keep it down."

When they stepped inside, he started to flip on the foyer light, then decided not to. It would shine up the stairs to the second story. Instead, he took Joy's cool, soft hand and led her through the darkness into the living room. Once again, her pale skin almost seemed to glow in the darkness. Her steps were silent.

He turned on the light beside the sofa. A dirty plate and glass, left over from his mom's supper or an evening snack, sat on the coffee table. Looking around his house like a newcomer would, Mike noticed the disarray. A spider had begun spinning a web around the plastic roses in the white porcelain vase, and the painting over the TV, a picture of a beach and heavy surf with storm clouds bunching overhead, needed straightening.

Joy looked around, frowning. Mike winced. His house truly wasn't tacky, but somehow, the small signs of neglect were enough to make it *seem* that way. "What do you think?" he asked reluctantly.

"I can see why you want to get away."

He felt himself blush. "It's not that bad."

"Of course not," she said soothingly. "It's just that it doesn't look very *interesting*. I think it's like school. You're outgrowing it."

He shrugged. "Well, I guess I'll be here till I go to college, whether I outgrow it or not. Do you want to watch TV? I think it'll be okay if we keep the sound down."

She strolled through the doorway into the dining room. "Hey, now we're cooking!" she said.

He followed her in, then peered around in the dimness. He couldn't see what she was so excited about.

"What is it?" he asked.

"Gas money."

For a second, he was still confused. Then he realized that she was looking at his mom's purse, sitting where it usually sat on a little marble-topped table.

"Sorry," he said. "Mom wouldn't give me an advance, especially if I woke her up to ask for it."

"So don't wake her."

"What? You mean—? No. No way."

Her eyes opened wide, as if she was surprised at his reaction. "We aren't going to have any fun here. I see now why you didn't want to come. We need to get back on the road."

"There are other things to do beside cruising."

"In this little town, after eleven on a Wednesday night? Like what?" She went on before he could think of an answer. "And how do you get to them with no car? Look, I'm not asking you to *steal*. Just *borrow* a few dollars until Saturday, then put back what you took."

"No. I can't."

She smirked. "What are you, chicken?"

"No," he said, frowning. "It just isn't right." For a heartbeat, he was mad at Joy. He even wondered why, or if, he really liked her.

Then her face fell. She looked so remorseful that he couldn't stay angry at her. "I'm sorry," she said. "I never should have said you were scared. You're going to hate me now, aren't you?"

"No!" he said. "Of course not."

She smiled sadly. "You're nice. I guess it is late. I think I will go home. It's not far. You don't need to drive me."

She started for the door, and as she did, she lifted the silver flask. Even in the dimness, the metal gleamed. It occurred to him that if she left, the gin would go with her.

46

Of course, it was a stupid thing to be thinking. It was his new girlfriend he cared about, not the liquor. And he sure didn't want her to go away upset. "Please, don't leave!" he said. "Look, I *don't* hate you and I'm *not* chicken and . . . I guess it wouldn't hurt to borrow a couple of dollars."

"Really?" she said. "Well, all right. If you're sure it'll be okay."

"I am." He turned and picked up the bag.

His fingers didn't seem to want to unzip it. In spite of what Joy had said, he knew that if he took any money, it *would* be a kind of stealing. Suddenly he had the feeling that today he'd been stepping over a series of lines, and every time he crossed one, he turned into a different person. When he'd drunk in the morning and at school, that had been one line. When he'd brushed off Karen and Pete, that had been another. And if he stole from his mom, that would be a third.

Did he *want* to cross it? Did he want to be the Mike Davis who was waiting on the other side?

No. He started to zip the purse back up. The floor behind him creaked.

He whirled. His mother stood before him in her pajamas, red flannel bathrobe, and slippers. Her pale blue eyes blinked as if the single lamp he'd switched on was too bright for her. Strangely, Joy was nowhere in sight.

Mike imagined how he must look, unsteady on his feet with the purse clutched in his hands. Probably he had a guilty look on his face and smelled like gin, too. He felt horribly ashamed. "Mom," he said. "I was just —"

"I came downstairs for some aspirin," she mumbled. "The medicine cabinet is out." She patted him on the arm, then drifted past him into the kitchen.

He stared after her, amazed. She hadn't noticed

47

that he'd been drinking or the purse either. At first he felt relieved, but by the time he heard her clumping back up the stairs, he began to get angry.

He was angry at his mom, for not caring enough about him to even really see him. Angry at Karen and Pete, for snooping into his business and telling him what to do. Angry at everyone who'd laughed at him today, or ever said anything nasty about his father. Suddenly he *wanted* to do things they wouldn't approve of. It would serve them right.

His mother had two twenties in her wallet. He took one. By the time he tossed the purse back on the marble-topped stand, Joy was standing beside him. He took the flask from her, threw his head back, and gulped down a long, long drink.

Eight

The next day Karen stood on the sidewalk looking up at Mike's house, wondering if she really wanted to go to the door. Even though he'd seemed funny yesterday and Anne had claimed he'd talked to a girl who wasn't there, Karen still could not believe that Mike was losing his mind. Heck, even if he didn't have good sense when it came to drinking and driving, he was one of the most normal guys Karen knew. He *must* have been putting Anne and the other kids on, and they just hadn't had brains enough to see through the act. He'd probably missed school today because he'd caught the flu. There was a bug going around.

But if Mike *didn't* believe that this Joy of his was real, why had he dumped Karen? She couldn't believe that he'd carry a joke that far.

Karen decided that she had to check on him. She wouldn't be able to stop worrying till she saw that he was okay. She straightened her shoulders, ran a hand through her red hair, marched up the drive, and rang the doorbell.

Chimes sounded faintly. She wondered who'd answer, Mike or his mother. Probably Mike; he'd said that his mom slept a lot, all through the day. A couple minutes dragged by, and she started to doubt that *anyone* was coming, even though both cars were in the garage. Finally, just as she was turning to leave, the door swung open. Mike squinted out at her.

She was shocked at his appearance. He was still wearing the same clothes she'd seen him in yesterday. His eyes were bloodshot; his face, pink and puffy. He smelled of sweat and alcohol.

"Hi," he said, sounding puzzled. "What are you doing here? Did you need a ride to school?"

"School's over," she said in amazement. Feeling as if she had to prove it, she stepped back, so he could look past her and see the sun setting behind the wooded hills west of town. "It's afternoon."

He looked at her suspiciously, as if he didn't believe her or his own eyes either. Then he nodded. "Oh, yeah. I think I remember Mom trying to get me up. I told her I was sick. What day is it, anyway?"

Karen wanted to scream at him: *What's the matter with you? What are you doing to yourself?* But if she blew up, he'd just get mad right back at her, and maybe slam the door in her face. If she wanted to find out what was going on with him, she'd have to ease into it. "It's Thursday, Mike. I went around to your teachers to get your homework."

"Thanks," he said. He hesitated, then shuffled backward. She followed him into the house.

He plopped down on the living room couch. She sat down beside him, opened her spiral notebook, and tore out the sheet on which she'd jotted down his assignments, not that it looked like he was in any shape to do them. "You seem a little out of it," she said.

He shrugged. "I'm still half asleep. You woke me up."

"Do you think you'll be able to go to school tomorrow?"

"Maybe. Who knows?" He ran his hand through his uncombed hair.

Abruptly Karen felt impatient. This was going nowhere. Tact was fine, but the only way to deal with a situation was to get it out in the open. "I'm worried about you," she said. "Tell me what's going on."

"What do you mean? I'm just sick."

"No, you aren't. I think you've been drinking again. A lot."

He squirmed. "You've got drinking on the brain."

"Are you telling me I'm wrong? I can smell it on you."

"All right, maybe I had a beer last night. So what? What makes it any of your business?"

For a second, she wanted to tell him that it *wasn't* her business, that she didn't care what happened to him, and leave. But she did care, so she held her anger in. "I'm trying to look after you. People notice you're acting funny."

He scowled. "If they were my friends, they'd mind *their* own business, too."

"Can't you tell that something's happening to you?" she demanded. "By being absent today, you missed the end of basketball tryouts. Pete says that unless Coach Yarborough gives you a break, you won't be a starting player."

For a heartbeat, he looked shocked, and she thought she'd gotten through to him. Then he grinned a nasty, crooked grin. "Big deal. It's just a stupid game. A kids' game. I've got better things to do anyway."

Only one more chance to jolt him back to his senses, thought Karen. It was time to talk about Joy. Karen realized that she'd been avoiding the subject because it was so weird, it would embarrass her to bring it up. "You never talked this way before. But okay, maybe you don't care about basketball any-

51

more. But you don't want to be crazy, do you?"

"What are you talking about now?"

She looked him in the eye. "Your new girlfriend. She isn't real. You're seeing things."

He laughed. "That's the lamest thing I ever heard. How gullible do you think I am?"

"Ask the other people at school."

"Sure. Like you haven't already made them promise to play along with the gag."

"Ask *anybody.*"

"And won't I look like a real Einstein doing it. Excuse me, can you see this girl standing beside me, or is she invisible to you? I was just wondering."

Karen's fingers fidgeted with the ends of her coppery hair. Why doesn't he believe me? She had a terrible feeling that Mike was going to be impossible to convince. "Does Joy *seem* real to you? All the time? Or have you noticed anything funny about her?"

For a moment, Mike looked confused. Then the confident sneer returned to his face. "She's different than other people I know, but I *like* the ways she's different. She understands me. She takes my side. We have fun."

Karen shook her head. "This is hopeless, isn't it? What's happened to you?"

"Nothing. Look, I appreciate you dropping by. The joke was hilarious, but I am sick, so maybe you should take off."

"All right," she said, standing up. As soon as she stepped onto the porch, the door thumped shut behind her, nearly whacking her on the butt.

Trudging back down the driveway, she tried to understand what she'd just seen. When they'd gone on their date, Mike had been a nice, normal guy.

Maybe he had a drinking problem, but he was still in the first stage of it. Except for making it dangerous for him to drive, it wasn't causing any difficulties.

52

Now, only a day and a half later, he was missing school, pushing away his friends, and slipping from reality.

Karen didn't know much about alcoholism, but she was sure Mike was going downhill too fast. It was as if the effects of years of problem drinking had happened to him in just a few days.

She shook her head. She couldn't sort it out. Then, as she reached the sidewalk, she sensed that someone was staring at her back.

She turned, expecting to see Mike looking down at her from the house. But all the windows were empty.

At least they were at first. Then a gray smudge appeared in the living room window. Her mouth dry, Karen peered at it, trying to make out what it was. At first she couldn't, and hoped it wasn't anything, just a trick of the light. But gradually it became clear, like an image on a screen when someone adjusts the projector. Now it was a pale, brown-haired girl in a funny-looking red dress.

Frightened, Karen gasped and stumbled backward. The girl in the window leaned forward, as if Karen's reaction had surprised her. Karen wheeled and ran.

Nine

Karen's dad cocked his head. The glow from the cut-glass fixture above the dining room table shone on his glasses, reminding Karen of the figure that had appeared in Mike's window.

She shivered, then realized her father had *spoken* to her. "I'm sorry," she said. "What did you say?"

Dad frowned. "I was talking about whether we should go to Miami to visit Grandma and Grandpa this Christmas. What were *you* daydreaming about?

"Mike Davis," said Paula, Karen's eight year-old sister. "Karen has the hots for him."

"Hush," said Mom. She didn't know what had happened on Karen's last date, but she'd seen her come home early and alone, and so realized she was in no mood to be teased about the boy she'd gone out with.

Karen cut a piece of meat off the baked chicken breast on her plate, then decided that she was too nervous to eat it. "I'm not very hungry tonight," she said. "May I be excused, please?"

Mom looked at her. "Do you feel all right?"

"I'm just tired," Karen said.

"Then why don't you lie down. I'll save your plate, so it'll be there later if you want it."

She sounded so kind that Karen wanted to tell her

what was wrong. But how could she, when she didn't know herself?

She climbed the stairs to her room, then lay down on the bed, shoving aside Mickey Mouse and Roger Rabbit to make room for herself. It would have been nice to nap, as her mother no doubt expected, but she couldn't get the events of the afternoon out of her mind.

Had she seen Joy? She'd been upset, and at least forty feet from the window. Maybe her nerves and the failing light had played tricks on her. But no. *She* didn't drink, *she* didn't see visions, and in the end, the brown-haired girl hadn't looked blurry at all.

Maybe there *was* a Joy, but she was just an ordinary flesh-and-blood person like everybody else. Mike had accused Karen of organizing a conspiracy to fool him, but maybe he, Joy, Anne, and the others were really playing an elaborate prank on *her.*

No, that didn't make sense either. Nobody would try to pull off a joke this peculiar and complicated. Mike certainly wouldn't blow off basketball just to spook her. And although she wasn't certain of much else, she was sure there was nothing phony about his drinking.

Well, if Joy was real, but not a normal person, what did that leave? Surely she wasn't a gh—

Beneath the window, a horn blared, breaking Karen's train of thought. It was just as well. She was so upset, she was imagining crazy things.

The horn blasted again. Curious as to why someone was making such a racket on her quiet little side street, she went to the window, pulled aside the sheers, and looked down.

A car sat idling in front of her house. It was night now, and the branches of the elm tree were half blocking her view, so she could barely make the vehicle out. But somehow, its shape was familiar, though she couldn't quite place it. She realized she didn't *want* to recognize it. She swallowed.

"Karen!" Mom shouted up the stairs. "There's a car outside. I think it's Mike's. Do you want me to go out and tell him you're not feeling well?"

Yes, Karen thought. "No!" she yelled. "I'll go out and see him." Because there had to be a logical explanation for everything that was happening. So she refused to cave in to fear. And if something horrible *was* going on, she couldn't let one of her family blunder into it when they didn't have a clue that anything was wrong.

She climbed slowly, reluctantly, down the stairs, then walked out into the night. When she'd gone a few paces, something behind her flashed. Startled, she jumped, then realized Mom had flipped on the porch lamp. That should have made Karen feel less jittery. But the darkness was pressing in around her, swallowing her, and the light didn't do anything to push it back. When she glanced back, the stoop looked a million miles away.

Ahead, the car's motor rumbled. White vapor blew out of its exhaust pipe, and its headlights burned like a leopard's eyes. The night turned its red paint black. Now Karen could make out the distinctive Mustang shape of it, but she couldn't see inside.

She took two more steps. A shadow appeared in the driver's seat. As far as Karen could tell, it was the only figure in the car.

Then everything's all right, she told herself, trembling. It's Mike's car, so if there's just one person inside, it must be him.

The shadow leaned past the gearshift and opened the door on the passenger side. The dome light came on. Revealing brown hair, fair skin, and a pretty, heart-shaped face. "Hop in," Joy said.

It's *still* all right, Karen insisted to herself. But her

instincts were screaming that no, there was something *wrong* with Joy, and at that moment, she couldn't have climbed into the Mustang if her life depended on it. She flinched backward, shaking her head.

Joy shrugged. "Suit yourself. We can talk standing up if you want to." She pulled the passenger door shut, then climbed out the other side of the car.

As the pale girl approached, Karen struggled not to run, to quash the panic in her mind. Darn it, Joy looked like an ordinary human being. What else *could* she be? "Hi," Karen stammered.

"Hi," Joy said. When she stepped close, Karen smelled perfume with a sharp, alcoholic scent beneath it, and noticed a tiny scar on the girl's forehead. "I guess we can skip introductions. I know Mike told you about me."

"Where is Mike?" Karen asked. "What are you doing driving his car?"

"He's taking a nap," Joy said, smirking. She means he's passed out, Karen thought. The idea made her mad, and the anger felt good because it pushed away some of her fear. "I knew he wouldn't mind if I borrowed this jalopy, and I thought you and I should talk. So I could tell you to stay away from him."

"Hey, Mike may be dating you," Karen said, "but he's been my friend ever since we were little, and I'm not going to stop hanging with him now. I couldn't avoid him if I did want to. We go to the same school, remember? We have a couple of the same classes."

Joy shook her head. "Wise up. He doesn't deserve your friendship. He could have killed you on the road."

Karen blinked, confused. Was Joy worried about Mike, too? "Then you see he has a drinking problem."

Joy giggled. "Oh, yes."

"Then we shouldn't waste time fighting over him or

dissing him either. We should be trying to figure out a way to help him."

The pale girl shook her head. "You don't get it. I want him drunk. I'm going to make sure he stays that way. I want him to crash his car and die. Or ruin his life at the very least."

Karen stared at her. "Are you kidding? That's horrible!"

Joy shrugged.

"It's also crazy!" Karen continued. "When the car wrecks, you'll probably be riding in it. You'll die too!"

Joy said, "No, I won't. Look, here's how it is. I came to push Mike over the edge. He was heading that way anyway. I'm not interested in you. But if I have to hurt you to get him, I will. So stay out of my way."

Karen shook her head. Her common sense told her that Joy *must* be joking, but somehow, she knew she wasn't. "Why are you doing this?" she whispered. "Who are you really? *What* are you?"

Joy smiled. "It's funny. You already know, but you don't want to know. You saw, but you won't admit it. I guess I don't blame you. What I am is dead already. I'll prove it."

She picked at the scar on her forehead like somebody scratching off a scab. Her pointed, red-polished fingernail broke the skin. Karen thought, please, I don't want to see this. But she couldn't look away.

Joy jabbed her nail into the wound, then pulled down, cutting her forehead, cheek, lips, and chin. The motion reminded Karen of somebody opening a zipper. The pale girl gripped her face with both hands, then pulled. The flesh tore apart around the gash, revealing the bloody skull beneath.

Shrieking, Karen turned and dashed for the house, certain every moment that Joy would grab her from

58

behind. Instead, a car door thumped shut. An engine roared, then rubber squealed.

Later that night Mike found himself cruising with Joy again. As usual they were having a good time driving and taking drinks from her silver flask.

Then his Mustang approached the railroad tracks just as the red warning lights began to flash. Bells clanged. Mike stepped on the gas, and the car surged forward. But not quickly enough. The striped crossing gate dropped in front of him. He hit the brakes. The car skidded to a stop right in front of the barrier.

"Go around," Joy said.

He turned and looked down the track. The train, a black hulk in the darkness, wasn't *real* close, nor was it moving very fast. Still, the thought of pulling out in front of it was scary. "You're not supposed to do that," he said.

"Oh, come on," Joy taunted. "You've got plenty of time. And look how long the train is. If we don't get across now, we'll be stuck here forever."

"If you don't want to wait, we can turn around," he said.

She pouted. "You said we were going to drive along the river. We can't do that if we go in the wrong direction."

He sighed. He should have known that he'd wind up doing what she wanted. He wondered again when, and *why,* he'd become so fond of her that she could wrap him around her little finger. But he guessed that if you had a sweet, beautiful girlfriend, it made sense to keep her happy. "Okay," he said.

He backed the car up a few feet, then swung around the gate onto the track. The locomotive's headlight glared through his side window. Its horn blew an angry-sounding blare.

Joy rested her fingertips on top of the dashboard.

The Mustang's engine stalled, leaving the car stuck in the middle of the track.

Mike stepped on the clutch, put the gearshift in first, then turned the key in the ignition. The starter groaned sluggishly without catching.

The train's horn blared again. Mike glanced up and was shocked at how much bigger it looked. He turned the key. The car didn't start. It sounded like the battery was even weaker now.

His heart thumped. He wondered if they ought to jump out of the car. But he couldn't stand the thought of losing it, or having to explain how it had been destroyed. Still, he ought to get Joy out of danger. "Get out!" he cried.

"I'm fine," she said, giggling. "It'll start next time."

She was being crazy, but there was no time to argue with her. He wrenched the key. The starter chugged once, then fell silent.

The train's brakes ground futilely. Mike looked around. The locomotive was only a few yards away. Now it was too late to scramble clear.

He sobbed, then noticed Joy's red-nailed fingers still resting on the dash. Giving in to a sudden impulse, he knocked her hand away, then turned the key.

The motor roared to life. The car lurched off the track, and the train howled by behind it.

Mike pulled over and put his face in his hands. Three near accidents in three nights. He didn't understand how it could be happening to him.

"You hit me," Joy said sullenly.

He lifted his eyes. For a second, the pale girl's expression looked more disappointed than angry. "What?"

"You slapped my hand," she said, holding it up for his inspection. "Why did you do that?"

He shrugged, confused. For a moment, it had seemed to Mike as if Joy's touch was keeping the engine from cranking. But, of course, that couldn't have been true. He'd just imagined it because he was so terrified. "I don't know. I'm sorry."

She frowned. "Well, kiss it. Make it better." He pressed her hand to his lips. Unlike his own fingers, hers weren't trembling, nor was her cool, soft skin sweaty. It was as if she hadn't been scared at all. "All right, I forgive you."

"How can you even be thinking about this when we almost got killed?" he asked.

"I'm not your little friend Karen," Joy said. "I know you can handle yourself."

"Right now I don't feel like it," he said. "Give me a drink, okay?"

"Coming up." She passed him the flask.

Ten

The next morning Karen headed straight for the school office. Karen winced when she saw Joan sitting at one of the desks behind the counter. With all that was weighing on her mind, she'd forgotten that her inquisitive friend worked here first period. People joked that she was the only one who knew how to run the computer.

Well, maybe one of the secretaries, dumpy, blue-haired Mrs. Hillyard or sultry Miss Gomez, whom half the boys were in lust with, would come and help Karen. No, no such luck. Joan spotted her and jumped up.

"What's up?" she demanded with a grin.

"I need to see Mr. Lamb," Karen said.

The tall girl raised her eyebrows. "Good grief, what for? Are you pregnant or something?" She smiled to show she was kidding.

Karen didn't like to lie, especially to a friend, but she also didn't want to explain. She didn't know who—or *what*—might be listening. "I want to talk about my SATs."

Joan cocked her head. For some reason, the gesture made her look like a long-legged bird. "Why? You did great on them." She lowered her voice. "It's really about Mike, isn't it?"

"No!" Karen said. The word came out too loudly. A couple of boys sitting in front of the vice principal's door—heaven only knew how they'd managed to get in trouble so early in the day — looked at her curiously. "I'm forgetting about Mike, just like you said I should."

"Uh-huh," Joan said skeptically. "You know, he's absent again today."

"I don't have time to talk," Karen said. "If I don't hurry, I'm going to be late. Can you just give me an appointment? During lunch, so I won't miss class." It occurred to her that, horrible as it was, Mike's problem must at least be helping her diet. The way she was skipping meals, surely she'd drop the ten pounds she'd been trying to lose.

"Whatever you say, Miss Mystery." Joan reached under the counter and brought out a clipboard. Karen hastily scribbled her name on the form attached to it. "Fifth period it is. Do you want a hall pass?"

"Thanks, but I can make it," Karen said. Gripping her clarinet case, she wheeled and strode for the door.

She supposed it was pretty crazy to talk to your guidance counselor because your boyfriend had fallen under the spell of an evil spirit. It would have been crazy even if she'd had the smartest counselor in the world, and Mr. Lamb was no brain surgeon. But she had to try *something*. Joy's little trick of peeling back her face had terrified her, but not so much that she was willing to step aside and let the pale girl destroy her friend. She wouldn't be able to live with herself if she did.

Of course, she didn't intend to tell Mr. Lamb that Mike was having trouble with a spook. He'd never believe it. But Joy's presence seemed connected to Mike's drinking. Maybe if Karen reported that he was turning into an alcoholic, and Mr. Lamb could somehow make him sober up, the spirit wouldn't be able to mess with him anymore.

Karen stepped into the corridor, rushed on toward the band room. Most kids had already gone into their first period classes, and the hall was nearly empty. She turned a corner, then froze.

One moment, the corridor before her was clear. The next, Joy was standing in front of the oil painting of Jeremiah Cooper and his fellow pioneers building log cabins. In the light of day, her image didn't look quite steady or quite solid. Something about it reminded Karen of how the illusion of water appears on a road on hot days.

George Naylor, a senior who played trombone, scurried out of the boys' restroom, then trotted on toward band. He passed within a foot of Joy, and it was obvious he didn't see her.

Joy smirked at Karen, saluted her with a silver flask, and drank. After a moment, she faded away.

Karen's heart thumped. Her knees felt rubbery. This doesn't mean I'm in trouble, she insisted to herself. Just because I saw Joy, that doesn't mean she knows what I'm going to do. She probably just appeared to me to make sure I'd stay scared. Now she's left, and I can go about my business.

Somehow Karen made herself creep on down the corridor, afraid every moment that the spirit would leap out of nowhere and grab her. A flowery scent, with a tang of alcohol underlying it, hung in the air near the painting. Holding her breath so she wouldn't have to smell it, she slunk on. Finally she reached the closed band room door. She could hear instruments sawing up and down scales and doodling snatches of melody.

Some of the tension quivered out of Karen's body. Perhaps she'd been in danger while she was alone in the hall, but surely nothing could happen to her in the middle of a crowd. She hurried inside.

Mrs. Rayburn, the music teacher, dressed in a pastel pants suit, lacy white blouse, and gold-rimmed glasses, said, "Miss Bradley. *Finally.* Thank you for working us into your busy schedule."

Some of the kids snickered. Blushing, Karen scrambled into her seat, opened her instrument case, and hastily put her clarinet together. As she wet her reed, Mrs. Rayburn tapped her baton, commanding everyone's attention. A moment later, they were playing.

Karen liked making music, and she tried to lose herself in the activity now. If she could, she wouldn't have to be afraid again until third period, when band and orchestra would both be over.

For a few minutes, it almost worked. Then Joy's image swam into focus behind Mrs. Rayburn. The spirit swung her flask back and forth in time to the beat.

Karen jumped. Her fingers slipped on the keys, and her clarinet squawked the wrong note. Anne Morgan glanced at her questioningly. The rest of the band played on, blind to the sneering figure before them.

Karen was scared, but once again, anger took a bit of the edge off her fear. So what if you're here? she thought. What can you do to me? Nothing, I bet. So I'm not going to let you shake me up. She grimly tried to concentrate on playing.

Something flicked against her lips. Surprised, she jerked the blackwood instrument away from her face and peered at it. As far as she could see, it looked the same as always. Maybe her nerves were playing tricks on her.

She started playing again. But suddenly the clarinet sounded wrong. *Clogged.* The keys resisted being pressed, humped up and down. White maggots wriggled out of the fingerholes and dripped from the bell.

This can't be happening, Karen thought, or everyone would see it. Joy's messing with my mind. If I use my willpower, I can make it stop.

More grubs writhed out of the clarinet's ebonite mouthpiece. Karen felt them squirming against her gums and on her tongue. She tasted their slimy foulness. One slipped and wriggled down her throat.

It was too much. She hurled down the clarinet, leaped up, and ran, retching, for the door.

Mrs. Rayburn darted toward her. Karen knew she wanted to help, but Karen couldn't let the woman touch her, because suddenly the teacher's curly, gray-streaked brown hair was covered with maggots, too. And Joy was slinking up behind her! Karen sidestepped Mrs. Rayburn's outstretched hands, then shoved her. The teacher stumbled backward and sat down hard on the linoleum floor, her mouth hanging open in surprise.

Karen wheeled, jerked open the door, and scrambled through. Joy was waiting on the other side. Her eyes were gone, the sockets full of grubs. "You can't run away from me," she said. "So let's be pals. Have a drink." She held out the flask. Fat pink earthworms squirmed from the neck.

Screaming, Karen ran down the corridor. Doors opened, and teachers, no doubt alerted by the noise she was making, lunged out and tried to grab her. She ducked around them and dashed on.

Her feet slipping, she staggered around a corner. A door to the outside appeared. Maybe if she got out of the building, she could lose Joy. She threw her weight against the door's release bar, hurling it open.

Suddenly, Karen found herself teetering on the edge of a sheer drop. The ground outside the door was gone, replaced by a huge rectangular pit, like an open grave. At the bottom, giant worms and serpents coiled. White, bat-winged things flapped out of the depths. Each had Joy's pretty, smirking face.

Karen felt herself begin to topple. Desperately, she threw herself backward—but stumbled into Joy's embrace. The pale girl tried to force the flask into her mouth.

Karen thrashed, broke free, but lost her balance. When she fell, she struck her head on the floor. The world turned mercifully black.

Eleven

Karen woke up squirming and kicking. Hands grabbed her. The restraint fanned her terror.

"It's all right, Karen!" said a woman's voice. "We just want to help you! It's all right now!"

It was the voice of Mrs. Plimel, the school nurse. Karen stopped struggling, then warily opened her eyes.

She was lying on the cot in the nurse's office. Mrs. Plimel, a chunky, round-faced woman in a spotless white uniform, and Mr. Lamb, a stooped, balding man with a thin little mustache, were the people holding her down.

Joy was nowhere to be seen. Karen relaxed slightly.

Mrs. Plimel and Mr. Lamb exchanged glances. The nurse nodded. Then the adults slowly released Karen. Their hands hovered, obviously poised to seize her if she resumed fighting, or tried to jump up and run away.

"Can you tell us what was wrong?" Mr. Lamb asked. His breath smelled like cigarette smoke.

Karen started to cry. "Yes!" she said. "Joy was after me! She made maggots come out of my clarinet, and her eyes, and Mrs. Rayburn's hair, and then she tried to throw me in a big grave!"

The two adults looked at each other again. "Then I can see why you were frightened," Mr. Lamb said slowly. "Anybody would be. But who is Joy?"

"I don't know," Karen said. "I mean, I know she's a spirit. At first only Mike Davis could see her, but now, for some reason, I can, too. She's trying to scare me so I won't mess up her plan."

Mr. Lamb nodded. "I see. What is her plan?"

"She's going to turn Mike into an alcoholic, so he'll get killed driving drunk. You've got to help me save him!"

"It would be terrible if that happened," the guidance counselor said. "Do *you* drink, Karen? Or does anyone in your family drink too much?"

"No," Karen said. She couldn't understand why he'd asked.

"Have you ever used drugs? You can tell me. I'm not going to call the police. I just want to help you."

Abruptly she understood that he didn't believe her. Of course he didn't. Karen had known no one would—that was why she'd decided to tell Mr. Lamb about Mike's drinking and not tell him about Joy. But now she was so terrified that she'd babbled the truth without thinking.

Well, maybe it would work out for the best. Heaven knew, she couldn't handle Joy by herself. She'd just have to *convince* Mr. Lamb. Why not, he knew that she was honest and sensible, and some people did believe in ghosts. Perhaps he was one of them.

"No, I don't do drugs," she said. "Mr. Lamb, please listen to me. I know what I'm saying sounds silly—"

The balding man smiled. "That's good, Karen. That's good insight."

"—but I can give you evidence"—she thought of Joan—"*data* to prove that something *strange* is going on."

"And I'll be interested to hear it," Mr. Lamb said soothingly. "But first, I think we ought to find out more about you. After all, you just had a nasty bump on the head. Have you ever injured your head before?"

"No!" Karen said. She didn't like the adults looming over her, so she sat up. The room tilted, and the back of her head throbbed. She winced.

"Go slowly," Mrs. Plimel said. She handed Karen a paper cup of water and two aspirin.

"I'm all right," Karen said. She swallowed the pain relievers. "Look, Mike's absent from school. Check on him. You'll find out that he's turned into a hardcore alcoholic faster than anybody *would* change, unless something unnatural made it happen."

Mr. Lamb leaned toward Mrs. Plimel and murmured behind his hand. Karen caught the words "confront the delusion."

The guidance counselor lowered his hand and smiled. "All right, Karen," he said. "If you think Mike has a drinking problem, I should certainly check on him." He scooted his wheeled chair to Mrs. Plimel's desk, flipped through the file cards in a metal box, then dialed the phone.

It took a long time for anyone to pick up on the other end. Finally Mr. Lamb said, "Hello, Mrs. Davis? This is Timothy Lamb, a guidance counselor at Mike's school. He's been absent, so I'm calling to check on him." A pause. "Uh-huh." Another pause. "I see. Well, um, this may seem like an odd question, but have you noticed any changes in his attitude or behavior lately?" He waited for the answer. "No, no reason, just making sure everything's all right. Have a nice day." He hung up the phone and looked at Karen. "Mrs. Davis says that except for the flu, Mike is fine."

For a second, Karen couldn't understand it. Then she remembered all that Mike had told her about his mom. "You have to understand, Mrs. Davis is depressed, at least I guess that's what you'd call it. She

69

sleeps all the time. So it's possible she wouldn't notice Mike's drinking."

"Uh-huh," Mr. Lamb said. "Now Mrs. Davis has a mental problem. Did spirits cause that one, too?"

"Spirits?" a man's voice asked.

It was Dad's voice. Karen's head snapped around. Her parents were standing in the doorway.

She leaped up and hurled herself into her father's arms. "Something terrible is happening," she said. "You guys have to believe me!"

"It's okay," Mom said, patting her shoulder. "We'll get it all sorted out."

"What's this all about?" Dad asked. "You were a little vague on the phone."

"First period, Karen flew into a panic for no apparent reason," said Mr. Lamb. "She screamed and ran out of the band room. When Mrs. Rayburn tried to stop her, so she could find out what was wrong, Karen knocked her down. Outside in the hall, she flailed around, fell, and hit her head."

"I had to run," Karen said. "Something was after me, something no one else could see. I know how that sounds, but it's true."

"Karen seems to think a spirit named Joy is persecuting her and Mike Davis," Mr. Lamb said. "Have you heard any of this before?"

"No," Mom said, frowning. "But last night, she ran into the house screaming. She said an owl swooped low and startled her, but I wondered."

Mr. Lamb nodded solemnly. "Does she have any psychiatric history?" he asked.

"No," Dad said. "She's always been—"

Karen couldn't stand the way they kept discussing her as if she weren't there. "Talk to *me!*" she cried.

Mom rubbed her shoulder. "All right, sweetheart, we will. Do you really believe a spirit is after you and Mike?"

70

"I don't just believe it, I *know!*"

Mom tried to smile. "You like Mike an awful lot, don't you, darling? It must have hurt when you realized things weren't going to work out."

Karen said, "I'm not imagining things! Joy is real! Other kids have seen Mike talking to what looked like an empty chair. Just ask them!"

Mr. Lamb sighed. "We already gave you one chance to prove your story. Considering the circumstances, one was enough. Mr. and Mrs. Bradley, I think we should talk privately. Karen, please, sit back down and wait with Mrs. Plimel."

Karen sat. She didn't want to, but she sensed that resistance would make her look even worse. The guidance counselor led her parents into the hall, where the three of them cast blurry silhouettes on the milky window in the center of the door.

Even Karen's mom and dad didn't believe her. She really couldn't blame them though. If she hadn't lived her story, she wouldn't have believed it either. But it still hurt, and it made her feel helpless and alone.

Snatches of conversation came through the door: ". . . obsessed with drinking . . . specialist . . . medication, or even brief hospitalization."

An icy thrill of fear shot through the teenager, almost as intense as the dread she felt of Joy. The adults didn't think she'd just had some kind of weird fit. They thought she had a true mental illness. They wanted her treated. Doped up. Locked up.

She wracked her brain, trying to figure out how to keep it from happening. Finally she got an idea. Frightened, angry, and hurt, she'd never felt less like laughing in her life, but she forced out a giggle anyway.

Mrs. Plimel stared at her. "What is it?"

Karen laughed louder. It had to look like she was overcome with mirth. At first the laughs were just

71

acting, but then she started to feel a crazy glee. She was in danger of becoming hysterical. She struggled to hang on to her self-control.

Mr. Lamb and her parents burst back into the room. "What is it?" Dad said.

She chortled, pretended she was trying to talk, chortled again, then gasped, "You all look so *funny!*"

Mr. Lamb peered inquiringly at Mrs. Plimel. She shrugged to show that she didn't know what Karen was talking about.

Mom caught on first. "Is this some kind of prank?" she asked. She spoke in her softest voice, the one that meant somebody in the family was really in trouble.

"Yeah," Karen said, stretching her mouth into a grin. "Somebody bet me I couldn't make you all think I was crazy. I won, huh?"

"For that you disrupted your class and knocked down a teacher?" Dad said, scowling. "And made your mother and me take off from work?"

"I'm sorry," Karen said. "I guess the joke got out of hand."

Mr. Lamb said, "Hold it. Karen truly seemed terrified before, and absolutely sincere when she told her story. What's more, she really did knock herself unconscious. Sometimes mentally ill people cover up their false ideas when they realize that others don't share them. I think it would be wise to go ahead and take her to Dr. Samuels."

Karen held her breath till Dad shook his head. "No. I guess you know psychology, but I know my daughter. She's not crazy." He glared at her. "But she sure as heck needs a lesson in consideration and responsibility. You, young lady, are grounded. And I certainly think the school ought to punish you, too."

Karen nodded meekly. She didn't mind being restricted. With Joy on the loose, she was afraid to

72

stray from home anyway. She wished she could help Mike, but she'd learned the hard way that she'd only ruin her own life if she tried. From now on, her friend was on his own.

Twelve

Later that same afternoon, Mike awoke abruptly from a nightmare. He'd been walking along train tracks when he heard the train chugging behind him. He began to run, but the train was coming closer. Bars had sprung up on either side of the tracks, making him a prisoner. Finally, he turned and was blinded by the locomotive's glaring headlight, baring down on him. The last thing he remembered was the sound of Joy's hysterical laughter and the screaming of the train's warning whistle.

He rubbed his tired eyes. He hadn't gotten to bed until nearly dawn and then he'd had nothing but bad dreams the whole time since. His head was pounding as he rolled out of bed, went to the bathroom, and showered.

It was just that near-accident last night that must have given me the bad dreams, he thought. Again, he couldn't recall much else about the night. He wondered, as the hot water pounded over his head, what was really happening to him. He needed to get out and cruise, he thought, to clear his head.

He quickly dressed in jeans, a shirt, and sweater and descended the stairs to find his mother watching television. He grabbed his jacket.

"Goin' out, Mom." He called, knowing that she wouldn't care anyway.

"Are you feeling better, dear?" she called, not even looking away from the game show.

"Yeah, yeah. I'll be back soon."

He walked to the car and was glad to see Joy leaning against his Mustang. How long had she been waiting for him? Had he made a date and somehow forgotten?

"Hello there, handsome," she said.

"Get in the car," he said, reaching for the door handle.

"Some greeting." She walked to the passenger side and slid into the seat.

"Sorry, I just want to get out of here." He started the engine, pulled out of the drive, and headed down the road.

At a stop sign, Joy turned on the radio then pulled out her flask. "You look like you could use a drink."

"Yeah."

She took a long swallow then passed it over to him. He lifted the flask and the enticing fumes of the gin tickled his nose. He tilted his head back. Man, could he use a drink.

No liquor came out of the bottle. "It's empty," he said in disbelief.

"It is?" Joy said. "I didn't realize I was taking the last swallow. Sorry."

He shook his head. He knew there was no reason for his amazement. Any bottle could be emptied, so why not this one? But this was the first time it had been drunk *dry*. In fact, now that he thought about it, *that* was the truly strange thing. In the past few nights, just how much gin had poured out of it? Surely, more than it could possibly hold.

Joy put her hand on his arm. "What's wrong?" she asked. "What are you thinking?"

His flash of fear faded. What *had* he been thinking? He couldn't quite recall, but he was sure it hadn't made any sense. "I don't know."

75

"Well, then, should we get moving?" Obediently, he put the car in gear. They drove for a long time in silence. And Mike found that just cruising wasn't fun anymore. He needed a drink to settle his jangled nerves. And to keep things lively. He didn't want to bore Joy. The other nights when he'd been sipping from the flask, they'd talked non-stop. Now that it was empty, he couldn't think of anything to say.

"We sure could use some more booze," she said.

He felt like she'd read his mind. "Yeah," he said glumly.

"So let's get some."

"At your place?" he asked, wondering if he was going to see her house at last.

"No. There's no more liquor at my home."

"I know a carryout in a nearby town where they hardly ever ID, but I don't have any more cash. Do you?"

She smiled. "Afraid not."

He glanced at her. "I can't take any more of Mom's money. She'd miss it for sure."

Joy said, "Forget it. Just turn in here."

"Here" was the parking lot of a combination super-market, pharmacy, and liquor store. Joy hadn't given him much warning; he had to jerk the steering wheel and cut across a lane of traffic to make it in the entrance. Horns blared behind them.

He pulled into a space. "Okay, we're here. Now what?"

"Now go in and get us something to drink. Just slip it under your jacket."

"You're kidding." But he could tell she wasn't. "No!"

"It's no big deal," she said. "Stores *expect* people to steal. They mark up their prices to balance it out."

"They also put shoplifters in jail."

76

"You're not going to get caught," she said. "You're too smart."

"Not as smart as you," he said. "Why don't *you* do it?"

"Because I'm the girl," she answered. "And you're the guy. You're supposed to take care of me."

He snorted. "I guess you aren't big on women's lib."

For a moment, she looked puzzled. "What? No. No, I'm not. But I'm big on you. I think you can do almost anything." She put her hand on his. "C'mon, won't you please get us a drink, so we can go on having fun?"

He opened his mouth to say no again. Then suddenly his head throbbed badly, and his stomach cramped. Somehow his hangover was abruptly worsened. He didn't understand how he could feel sick so suddenly, only that he needed another drink to make himself well.

But stealing was wrong. A part of him still regretted taking his mom's money last night. And stealing from a store was wrong and stupid. "Sorry," he said. "I just can't."

"All right," she sighed. "I shouldn't have pushed you. It's just that I feel so shaky, and I need another drink to calm down. But I guess that's *my* problem, right?" She leaned against her door and looked straight out the windshield. He felt as though an invisible wall had risen between them.

Combined with misery in his head and guts, her sudden coldness was more than he could stand. "I'll go in," he said. "If I think I can sneak something out, I will. But if it looks like I might get caught, I won't."

"Thank you," she said, her black eyes shining. She kissed him. Her lips were pleasantly cold, like a touch of ice when he was hot and sweaty, and he relished the taste of gin that clung to them. For a moment, his headache eased.

He got out of the car and walked up to the brick

building. The liquor store was separate from the rest of the grocery, with its own entrance. The automatic door swung silently open.

He walked into the store trying to look as if he belonged there. The clerk behind the counter, a short, pot-bellied guy in a white, short-sleeved shirt and striped tie, didn't look up from the magazine he was reading.

Mike slunk up and down the aisles. After what seemed like hours, he found the gin.

He glanced around. There were curved surveillance mirrors hanging just below the ceiling, but the clerk still had his nose buried in his reading. So Mike reached for a green bottle of a brand called Tanqueray. Then he hesitated.

Did he really want to risk going to jail? Making his mother and friends ashamed of him? Messing up his future? For what, Joy? Sure, he liked her, but he'd only known her for a few days. For a drink? Drinking was fun, but he didn't *need* it. Did he?

He started to turn away. The gin bottles glittered in the fluorescent light. He stared at them. After a moment, he smelled the pine-needle scent of the liquor inside, even tasted it on his tongue. He knew it was just his imagination, but the sensations were as keen as real ones. They made him want a drink even more than before.

He decided he *would* take a bottle. Joy was right, he was smart enough to get away with it, no sweat. And if he did get caught, well, he was a juvenile. The court would let him off with a slap on the wrist. And what did it matter what his mom and so-called friends thought? They didn't really care about him anyway.

He picked up the green bottle and slipped it under his pale blue denim jacket. A hand fell on his shoulder. He jumped, squawked, and lost his grip on the gin. It fell and shattered on the linoleum floor.

"Oh, great!" growled a deep voice. The hand spun him around.

Mike found himself looking up at a tall, broad-shouldered man with a mole at the corner of his mouth. The badge clipped to his breast pocket read, BILL COPE, DEPT. MANAGER. Mike couldn't understand why he hadn't spotted him before. Maybe he'd just come out of the stockroom.

Mike's eyes felt hot and wet. His bladder ached, and for a second, he was afraid he was going to pee his pants. "Wait," he said, "this isn't how it looks! I — "

"I'm sure," Cope said. He turned his head toward the front of the store. "Hey, Walt! I caught a shoplifter. Underage, too. Call the police."

Mike shuddered. How could this be happening? What had he been thinking? What was the matter with him?

All he knew was that he couldn't let himself be arrested. Since Cope's head was still turned, maybe he could break away from him. He punched him in the gut.

The manager gasped. His grip loosened. Mike tore free, pivoted, and ran for the door.

His foot slipped in the spilt gin. Flailing his arms, he barely managed to avoid a fall. By the time he recovered his balance, Cope was scrambling after him. And Walt was emerging from behind the counter to block the exit.

Mike ran. When he reached the intersection of two aisles, he faked right, then dashed left, adding another second to his lead.

But Cope's feet still pounded close behind him. Mike began raking his hand along the shelves, hurling bottles to the floor. Maybe the broken glass and slippery puddles would slow his pursuer down.

He turned another corner, saw that Walt wasn't guarding the door anymore, but running dow aisle at him. Mike hesitated, and Cope grabbed him again.

The manager was panting. His face was red, and his free hand was clenched into a fist. He looked so angry that Mike was terrified he was going to beat him.

The boy snatched a brown bourbon bottle off a shelf, lashed it at his captor's head. Cope whipped his arm up to block, but too slowly. The bottle thudded against his temple.

Now Cope did punch at Mike. The blow only grazed his cheek, but it stung. Sobbing, the boy swung the bottle again. It struck Cope's forehead and the bottom half of it smashed, cutting him. Amber whiskey and shards of glass showered over them both.

Staggering, Cope let Mike go. The teenager wheeled and charged straight at Walt, holding the jagged-edged bottle neck in front of him like a sword. The short man stood his ground for another moment, arms extended to grapple, then jumped aside, and let him pass.

Mike noticed that he was beside the gin shelves again. He grabbed another green bottle, then dashed on out into the parking lot.

He hurled himself into his seat and slammed his door. Thrusting the Tanqueray into Joy's hands and throwing the car into gear, he zoomed back onto the street and away.

Joy grinned at him. "How was it?"

For a second, he wanted to slap her. "Oh, terrific! I almost got caught!"

She opened the gin bottle and passed it to him. "But you didn't. You were too smart and too fast, just like I knew you would be."

He swigged from the bottle. Warmth glowed in his stomach. The tension began to ease out of his muscles. He drank again. "You don't understand. I *hurt* somebody." The thought horrified him.

"Bad?" she asked.

"I don't know. I guess not. He was cut, but I didn't bash in his skull or anything." He took another drink. His hands stopped shaking.

"I'll bet it was self-defense, wasn't it?"

Mike blinked in surprise. Since he'd been a thief and Cope had been trying to catch him, he hadn't thought about it that way. But . . . "Maybe you could say that. It seemed like he was going to punch me out."

She shrugged. "Well, then, what are you feeling bad about?"

Was he dumb to feel guilty for hurting Cope? Suddenly, he didn't know. "I did a lot of damage in the store, too."

"I'm sure you didn't do enough to put the company out of business, so who cares? Come on, stop whining and tell me the story. I bet it was a real adventure, wasn't it?"

An adventure. Well, now that Joy was gazing at him admiringly, and his fear had passed; and now that he had something to drink, Mike could see that maybe it had been an adventure. Maybe it had even been fun, the same kind of scary fun as a rollercoaster. It must have been, because he was feeling a rush, like the exhilaration that came from winning a hard-fought basketball game.

"It was exciting," he admitted, lifting the Tanqueray bottle. "A *once*-in-a-lifetime experience, because I'm sure not doing it again."

"Of course not," Joy purred. She clinked the silver flask against the stolen fifth, then took a drink.

A thrill of fear shot through him. He hadn't seen her refill the flask from the green bottle. But of course she must have, or it wouldn't have anything in it. He just hadn't noticed. The suspicion that there was something *wrong* with her faded from his mind.

81

Thirteen

It was Friday night, and Karen sat on her bed, watching the swaying elm tree and the dark empty street beyond her window. When she sensed eyes gazing at her, she gasped. Frightened, she lurched around.

Someone *was* staring at her, but it was only Paula, looking in from the hall. Startled by Karen's sudden motion, the eight year-old flinched. Her pigtails, a slightly less bright and coppery red than her sister's, bounced on her shoulders.

Karen made herself smile. "Sorry. I didn't mean to scare you. What's up?"

"Did you really hit a teacher today?" Paula asked, her eyes enormous. It was obvious she couldn't believe that anyone, particularly the sister her parents generally held up to her as an example, could commit such a hideous crime.

Karen felt an urge to explain what had really happened. Telling might ease the fear still seething inside her. But it might also make Joy come after her, for daring to blab her secrets. And certainly, Karen couldn't expose a little kid to the danger that knowing those secrets might bring. "I didn't hit her, I just pushed her," she said wearily. "I didn't mean to. I was goofing around, and things got out of hand."

"Wow," said Paula. Then, gloatingly, "You must be

retarded. Dad told Mom you ought to stay grounded till *Christmas*."

"Get out of here," Karen said, annoyed. She pitched her stuffed Roger Rabbit at Paula. Giggling, the younger girl ducked, then disappeared down the hall.

Karen turned back to the window. Her white, haggard image reflected against the glass. Beyond it, the sky was black. She imagined Mike driving somewhere in the darkness, drunk, dazed, and helpless with a dead thing at his side, and whimpered.

She cared about him so much. She'd liked him ever since first grade, when he'd punched out the bully who had been throwing iceballs at her, and they'd shared a thousand good times since. Hanging together on a field trip to the New York Museum of Natural History—gaping at the dinosaur skeletons and the whale hanging from the ceiling; watching last year's pro basketball playoffs on the TV in her family room—ordinarily, she wouldn't have cared about the games, but his excitement made them fun; swimming and playing tennis last summer—when he'd first held her hand.

But it wasn't like Karen had *abandoned* Mike. She'd *tried* to help him and found out that she couldn't. If she got involved in his problem again, Joy would just ruin *her* life, maybe even kill her, without it doing anyone any good. So she *wasn't* being a coward, only sensible.

She wanted to stop thinking about Mike. She'd gone through the rest of the day like a zombie, trying to steer clear of the gossip. And now she just needed something to distract her from thinking about him and his problem. But she knew she wouldn't be able to concentrate on a book, and Dad had forbidden her to come downstairs to watch TV, or even play her stereo. For a second, she was tempted to close her door and listen with headphones. But the way her luck was running, she'd get caught, and wind up restricted for the rest of her life.

She realized that her parents couldn't object to music if she made it herself. If she practiced her clarinet, she was doing homework. Fortunately, the instrument hadn't broken when she'd thrown it. She set the case on the bed and tried to open it.

Her hands shook.

I'm being stupid, she thought. The maggots weren't real, and Joy isn't here. Still, as she fumbled with the clasps, she was poised to snatch her arms back, in case grubs writhed out as soon as she cracked it open.

They didn't. There was nothing inside but the gleaming black-and-silver sections of the instrument.

All right, stupid, she said to herself, now you see that everything's all right. So relax. But she didn't. Because last time the maggots had appeared without warning, when she had already had the clarinet in her mouth.

Still trembling, she put the woodwind together, then wet the reed. A rotten taste clung to it. She told herself it was just her imagination. She gasped in a ragged breath and tried to play.

Something squirmed against her lips. The keys wiggled of their own accord. She wailed and flung the clarinet on the bed.

There was nothing wrong with it. Fear had only made her think there was.

Suddenly she sensed that if she let Joy win, if she let terror rule her, she'd never play the clarinet again. She'd be scared to. And scared of the dark. Scared to go to school. Scared of strangers. Fear would cripple her till the day she died.

No! She wouldn't let that happen! She *had* to help Mike, for *both* their sakes, no matter how dangerous it was. She grabbed the clarinet, stuck it back in her mouth, and blew.

The first tone was a weak, wavering moan. She drew

a deep breath and tried again. The next note was steadier. Soon she was blasting out long, loud howls mixed with fast, skirling patterns of notes. The angry sounds made her mad, too, pushing the fear out of her mind.

When she finally lowered the clarinet, she was grinning fiercely. The smile slipped when she realized she didn't know what to do next.

How was she supposed to help Mike, when he wouldn't listen to reason, and his would-be killer was a spook that only the two of them could see? What could anyone do against a ghost?

Perhaps her first move should be to find out more about Joy. Unfortunately, she didn't know how to do that, either.

Wait. Hadn't Mike said he and the spirit had met outside the Night Owl, or, as all the kids had begun calling it, the Nightmare Club? Maybe if Karen poked around there, she'd learn something. She couldn't imagine what, but at this point, any plan was better than none.

She put the clarinet back in its case, prepared for bed, and flipped off the light. Tomorrow night she would sneak out to the club.

Fourteen

Saturday evening Mike awoke feeling sick. His guts churned, and his head pounded. His muscles ached. As he painfully sat up in bed, he noticed he was still wearing the clothes he'd put on yesterday afternoon. The ones he'd robbed the store in.

Robbed the store in? That couldn't be right! He strained to remember what had really happened. His pulse beat in his neck and wrists. Cold sweat oozed from his pores.

At first his memory was faint, like a dream that begins to fade as soon as the dreamer wakes, and he dared to hope the robbery *hadn't* happened. Then the image of a green bottle flashed into his mind. His recollections sharpened into clarity.

Yes, he'd done it. Shoplifted, destroyed things, and hurt somebody. How could it have happened? And how could he possibly get away with it? What if the salesclerks had given the police a good description of him? What if the cops had already started looking for him?

He needed to feel better, needed to calm down. If he weren't so sick and scared, maybe he'd be able to figure out what to do.

And of course he knew what he needed in order to

brace himself. The remembered taste and scent of gin flooded his mouth and nose. But there wasn't any alcohol in the house. He'd just have to hope that Joy brought some over.

He got up and staggered down the hall toward the bathroom, pulling off his stinking, wrinkled clothes as he went. Gradually it dawned on him that not enough light was coming in the windows, and most of what there was, was shining on the west side of the house. It was dusk, not morning.

Fear rose into his throat and choked him. He hadn't meant to sleep through yet another day. Suddenly he had the feeling that his whole life was sliding out of control.

I've got to get my act together, he thought, stumbling into the shower. Maybe I should rest tonight, not go out. Then he remembered Joy's pretty face, her teasing voice, the cool, gin-flavored touch of her lips, and realized that he wanted to see her too much to stay away. He needed her affection and admiration.

But did they *have* a date for tonight? He couldn't remember making one, any more than he remembered dropping her off anywhere last night or even the night before. He'd just have to hope so.

When he shaved, his hand shook, and he gashed his face twice. With bits of toilet paper stuck to his face, he pulled on his clothes and crept downstairs.

His mom was sprawled on the living room couch, her head thrown back. Soft snoring buzzed from her mouth.

Mike's stomach rumbled. He felt queasy, not hungry, but he had a feeling that he ought to eat. He turned toward the kitchen, then something tapped him on the shoulder.

He whirled. Joy stood before him, smirking, no doubt at his alarm.

"What are you doing here?" he asked.

87

She said, "I'm here for our date, silly. The door was unlocked."

Maybe it had been, but he couldn't believe she'd opened it and crossed the foyer without him hearing. Suddenly he remembered Karen's weird put-on the other day. He wondered if maybe it hadn't been a joke after all. If he woke up his mom now, would she be able to see Joy? Trembling, he fell back a step.

"You look nervous," Joy said. She held out the flask. "Have a drink."

A part of his mind told him not to take it. If there was something wrong with Joy, it was crazy to drink something she gave him. But he wanted the gin too badly to refuse. He accepted the flask, glanced at his mother, making sure she was still asleep, then gulped down several mouthfuls.

The liquor relaxed him, driving his crazy suspicions out of his mind. By the time he lowered the bottle, he could barely even remember being scared of her.

"Let's hit the road," she said.

Once they were rolling, he asked her, "Do you think the police are looking for me?"

She grinned. "Sure. Thousands of them, with tommy guns and bloodhounds."

He glared at her. "I'm serious!"

"Then no. If the cops had identified you, don't you think they'd know your address? They would have come to your house by now. You're in the clear." She handed him the flask.

He tried to stay upset. It seemed like he still *ought* to be upset. But when he took a drink, relaxation tingled through him, while worry and irritation slipped away. In their place grew a guilty pleasure. Sure, he was ashamed of what he'd done, but it was still exciting to think that he'd done something so daring, so forbidden, and gotten away with it. "I hope you're right," he said.

"In a way, I almost wish the cops *were* after you," she said wistfully. "Then you'd have to run away, and we'd spend our lives together on the road."

"That's a weird idea," he said. But actually, the thought of it appealed to him. After all, the time he spent cruising with her was the only part of his life he enjoyed anymore. His old friends had blown him off, and his old interests seemed boring and unimportant. "We wouldn't have any money to live on."

She took the flask back and drank. "You could get it. As good as you drive, you could make more than you'd know what to do with."

"How?" Mike asked skeptically.

Joy touched her fingertip to the dashboard. "Have you ever raced this thing?"

It was time for Karen to put her plan into action. With luck, her parents would think she was asleep. She opened her window and crawled out onto the nearest branch of the elm.

Even in the dark, descending was easy. She remembered every hand and toehold from climbing the tree as a tomboy at Paula's age. For a moment, she was sorry that time in her life was over. Her life had been a lot less scary then. It had been a lot less scary a week ago, she thought to herself. She dropped lightly to the ground, then jogged down the street.

A few minutes later, she strode across a highway into a vacant lot. A black mass of trees reared up ahead. Since she didn't have a car, there was no point taking the road to the club. For a person on foot, the quickest route was the path through the woods.

Fifteen

The Mustang sped toward a bend in the two-lane road. Mike hit the brakes a little too late, and the car took the curve too fast. For an instant, it looked like they might slide partway off the road, or even side-swipe the steel guardrail. Then Mike yanked the wheel. Tires squealing, the Mustang swerved back into its lane.

Mike's heart thumped. Tension buzzed along his nerves. He liked it. Now that the crisis had passed, the feeling was exhilarating. Laughing, he said, "Let me have a drink."

Joy handed him the flask. For some reason, his hand was slightly numb, and he almost dropped it. Whoa, he thought. Wreck the car if you have to, but don't spill the gin. The thought seemed hilarious. He laughed again, then said, "Are you sure guys race on Old Wilson Highway?"

"No," the pale girl said, "but they used to, so maybe they still do. At least it'll be fun to find out."

" 'Used to,' when?" Mike asked. "And how do you know?" Joy had said that until a few days ago, she'd been gone from the Hollow for a long time. Surely she hadn't known anything about drag racing when she was a little girl.

"Years ago," she said. "I heard about it." Her vague answers left him confused. But he was getting used to feeling that way. It no longer bothered him that there were things about her he didn't grasp.

"You understand, I'm not going to race," he said. "I just want to watch."

"Sure," she said. She took the silver flask, drank, and handed it back.

Actually, he wasn't being honest. He thought he might race. Why not? He felt good tonight. Sharp. Confident. He could probably drive as competitively as he played basketball. But he was reluctant to admit he was considering it for fear that, if she knew, she'd pressure him. If she did, he knew he'd probably give in, even if it no longer seemed like a smart idea.

The Mustang bounced in a pothole, lashing the plastic dinosaur back and forth on the end of its cord. From the corner of his eye, he saw Joy stiffen. He opened his mouth to apologize for the jolt. Before he could, she said, "Turn around."

"What?" he asked, surprised.

"Turn around," the pale girl repeated coldly, taking the gin back. "I need to get back to the Hollow. Some-body's poking her nose in my business. I gave her fair warning, and now I'm going to *fix* her."

"Is this some kind of joke?" Mike asked. He had no idea what she was babbling about, and this time, it *did* bother him.

Perhaps Joy realized how vicious and crazy her face looked, because she managed to smooth it into a smile. "I'm sorry," she said. "I had a problem with somebody yesterday, and it's been bothering me ever since. I hate to spoil our date—you know I love being with you—but I won't be able to enjoy *anything* until I sort the situation out. So would you hate me if we call it a night?"

"Did you have trouble with somebody at school?" he asked. Sometimes new kids got hassled. The thought of somebody, maybe one of the same people who'd given him a hard time, bothering her made him mad. "They all know me. If you're going to talk to one of them, let me go with you."

"This is nothing you can help with," she said. She laid her hand on his arm. For a moment, he felt dizzy. "Please, just take me back to town."

"All right," he said. He wished she'd tell him more, but she obviously didn't want to. And he didn't want to push her, or delay doing what she asked, for fear that she'd get upset with *him*.

The road was so narrow that he had to creep through the Y-turn to avoid dumping the Mustang in the ditch. Joy kept smiling, but her white, red-nailed hands opened and closed impatiently.

Finally they were speeding back toward the Hollow. The car crested a hill, and the town's lights shone below them. "Where do you want me to drop you?" he asked, wondering if he was finally going to see her home.

"Cross Road," she said. "Step on it, please!" He did. He doubted she really needed to be in such a hurry, but it was fun to drive fast, so why not? A minute later, they were careening down Thirteen Bends, the steep road with its notorious thirteen hairpin turns. People said that Thirteen Bends had at least one fatal car crash every year. For a moment, the thought chilled him. Then he snorted and pushed it out of his mind.

He skidded around a corner. Ahead, his lights revealed the nameless turnoff that led to the Nightmare Club. They weren't far from Cross Road.

"Turn here!" Joy said. He stamped on the brake pedal. The Mustang fishtailed. "No, keep going!"

"Make up your mind," he said, momentarily annoyed. He jerked the wheel and stepped on the gas. The car shot forward.

Ranks of trees slid by on either side. After another minute, Joy said, "Stop."

He started to slow down, but he also stared at her in disbelief. "Is this a joke? We're in the middle of the woods. There's nothing here."

"So much the better," Joy said.

"What?"

She smirked at him. "Nothing. Look, this really is where I need to be. See you tomorrow." She caressed his cheek.

He realized that for the last few seconds he'd been looking at her, not the road. He peered forward, finished stopping the car, then turned to her again.

For a second, he thought he saw a shadow sitting in her place. Dark eyes shone in the middle of its otherwise featureless head, and the curves of its torso reflected the light from the dashboard, just as Joy's shiny red dress had. Then it faded away, leaving the seat empty.

Yelping, he cringed back against his door. The shadow wasn't there, he told himself. My eyes were playing tricks on me.

But if it hadn't been real, what had happened to Joy? After a moment, he decided she must have jumped out and disappeared into the trees while his head was turned. Even though he hadn't heard the car door click open and thump shut. Even though the Mustang had only been stopped an instant. Because it would be stupid to imagine anything else. He didn't *want* to imagine anything else.

He tried to think of something to do that would be fun even without Joy and the gin. Nothing came to mind. He drove home and staggered up to bed.

Sixteen

Karen scurried along the path. Trees pressed close on either side, sometimes tripping her with their roots. Whenever she heard a noise, the hoot of an owl or the grumble of traffic on the highway, she jumped. She kept hoping she'd catch up with some other kid on his way to the Nightmare Club, but so far, she seemed to be alone in the woods.

That's right, she thought, annoyed with herself. Alone is *exactly* what I am. Joy's off joy-riding with Mike. So it's stupid to be scared.

She heard a soft sound behind her. The fine hairs on the back of her neck stood on end. She whirled.

And saw nothing. But though she hadn't quite recognized the sound, she sensed that a person coming down the trail had made it. If she waited for him, she wouldn't be by herself anymore.

So she stood and gazed down the path. Her pulse beat in her neck. Her mouth tasted rusty with fear.

This is *really* dumb, she thought. Why do I feel even more scared than before?

Because, her intuition was screaming, that the person — or *thing* — approaching meant to hurt her. But Karen didn't believe in intuition, and she'd promised herself she wouldn't panic again. She struggled to stand her ground.

And did. For five heartbeats. Then fear overwhelmed her. She darted off the path and crouched behind an oak.

A shadow appeared on the path. A shaft of moonlight shone on brown hair and a slender white arm. Karen shuddered and bit her lip. A part of her mind desperately insisted that the figure might not be Joy. Other kids had brown hair and fair complexions. Then it paced closer, and she saw its sneering, heart-shaped face and silky red dress.

Karen held her breath, attempted to stay absolutely still. Fear tried to close her eyes, and she fought to hold them open.

Joy stalked closer. Her body seemed to flicker, as if she were moving under a strobe light. Then she stopped, frowned, and peered about.

I'm going to scream, Karen thought. I can't hold it in. Then the ghost strode on, disappearing down the trail a moment later.

Karen shuddered. All right, she thought, now I can run home. Then she realized that, even with Joy in the woods, she didn't want to. If the ghost had decided to keep her away from the Nightmare Club, then maybe that was where she needed to be. So darn it, she was going to get there!

But she couldn't use the path, not with Joy prowling on it. Doing her best to move silently, she crept farther away from the trail. When it was out of sight, she started slinking toward the club, peering warily about, wincing every time her tread snapped a twig, or crunched fallen leaves.

For a minute, nothing happened, and she dared to hope she wouldn't have any further contact with Joy. Then a voice sang out: "K — a — a — r — e — n!" She froze.

"I told you, I'm not after you," the spirit continued. "So talk to me. If you'll just promise to mind your own business, I'll leave you alone." No, you won't, Karen

95

thought. You wouldn't be dumb enough to believe me. "If you won't promise, if you make me keep chasing you, then I'm going to hurt you when I find you. And I will find you. I can feel you with my mind. That's how I knew what you were up to in the first place."

I guess you can sense things about me, Karen thought, but you can't zero in on my exact location, or you would have found me already. So no way am I giving up. You'll have to catch me. She crept on.

Joy kept calling her name. At first, the living girl was glad, because she thought the shouts would help her keep track of the spirit's position. Then she noticed that sometimes the calls came from the right, sometimes, the left. One moment they sounded in front of her, the next, behind. It didn't seem possible that the ghost was flitting around so quickly, crossing and recrossing Karen's path without either of them glimpsing the other.

Abruptly, Karen realized there was another explanation. If the cries seemed to come from different directions, it might mean she was moving in circles. And if she was blundering around aimlessly, then Joy was sure to find her sooner or later.

Karen peered wildly about. She'd explored this patch of woods many times, but suddenly, nothing looked familiar. She *was* lost. Her only chance was to run—

No. She mustn't panic. If she bolted, she'd make noise. Joy would hear and catch her. Karen had to remember, the spirit could confuse her senses, and that was probably what was happening now. No matter what direction the cries seemed to be coming from, no matter how unfamiliar her surroundings looked, she didn't think she'd gotten turned around. The Nightmare Club should still be ahead of her. She skulked on.

After another minute, speed-metal music whispered through the trees. Elated, she pushed forward, through another thicket. When she emerged, she saw a square black mass that could only be the Nightmare Club squatting among the trees. To someone else, the dark, hulking building might have looked frightening, but to Karen, it was a vision of salvation. Grinning, she dashed forward.

Joy stepped from a patch of shadow a few yards ahead and to her right.

There was no way Karen could dash straight to the door. Joy would intercept her. Her only chance was to run around the Nightmare Club, hoping to find another entrance. She sprinted to her left.

She fought the urge to glance back. It would slow her down. But it was horrible, not knowing how fast Joy was gaining on her. She strained to hear the ghost girl's footsteps, but couldn't.

She rounded the side of the building. No doors, just windows. Certain she couldn't open one and clamber inside before Joy caught up with her, she dashed on. By the time she reached the rear of the club, she was gasping.

But in the center of that wall was the back door. She ran for it, tripped over a bump in the ground, and started to fall. Flailing her arms, she somehow managed to stay on her feet. She scrambled on, grabbed the brass doorknob, and twisted it.

It wouldn't turn. The door was locked.

Refusing to accept that it wouldn't open, she tore at the knob, pounded the wood, and shrieked, "Let me in!" Something white winked at the corner of her eye. Her head snapped sideways, and she saw Joy rounding the corner of the building. The pale girl looked as if she was only striding, but somehow, with her flickering gait, she was moving faster than Karen could run.

Sobbing, Karen dashed on. Turned another corner. No door.

She reeled down the side of the building. Horribly,

she realized that, despite her terror, she was beginning to slow.

But somehow she neared the front of the club without Joy stopping her. I might make it! she thought with giddy disbelief.

Unless Joy had raced back the way they'd come. Unless she was waiting around the turn.

Now Karen wanted to look back more than ever. But she still didn't dare.

She staggered around the corner. For a moment, in the darkness, her eyes blurry with sweat and tears, she thought she was alone. Then a hand closed on her forearm.

Seventeen

Karen thrashed, and tried to lash out with her free hand. Fingers locked around her wrist. "Hey!" said a woman's voice. "Take it easy. I'm a friend."

It wasn't Joy's voice. Blinking the tears and sweat out of her eyes, Karen saw a slender young woman with ash-blond hair. The ghost was nowhere in sight. Maybe Joy was unwilling to kill a victim in front of a witness. After all, if someone saw Karen die a mysterious death, people might decide her spook story had been true after all. Her terror eased a little. "Something, I mean, I *thought* something was following me."

"Then we'd better call the police," the blond woman said.

"No!" Karen said. If the cops got involved, her parents would find out she'd sneaked out. "I bet nothing was really there. I didn't *see* anything. Couldn't we just go inside and forget it?"

The blonde shrugged. "Maybe. If that's what you want." She gazed into the darkness, then murmured something under her breath. More of Karen's fear slipped away. She didn't know why, but she had a feeling that if Joy had still been lurking nearby, she wasn't anymore. The blonde gestured toward the door. "After you."

When they stepped inside, Karen saw that a lot of kids were spending Saturday night at the club. Evidently Spider Game, one of the best local bands, had just finished their first set, because they were stepping off the stage. Couples were leaving the dance floor, drifting back to their tables and booths.

Abruptly, Karen felt like crying. All the other kids were smiling and laughing. They looked carefree. Unafraid. She wished she could be like them.

A white-haired man with a hooked beak of a nose walked up to the blond woman. "What was it?" he asked.

She shrugged. "Something scared my new friend here. What, I don't know. I'm going to sit with her a little while, okay?"

"Now," the old man said. "When the band's on break, and everyone wants to order. Fine, go ahead, I'll do everything as usual." He stalked away.

Karen said, "I'm all right. You don't have to—"

"Don't be silly," the blonde said firmly. "Come this way." She led Karen toward the bar at the back of the room. Spotting the redhead, several kids from Cooper High shouted jokes about her being crazy. Blushing, she made herself grin. She knew that if she showed the teasing bothered her, they'd keep it up forever.

The blond woman installed her on a stool, moved behind the polished oak bar, and poured two Cokes. "Introduction time," she said. "I'm Jenny Demos. My father and I own the club."

"Karen Bradley," the teenager replied. They shook hands.

"If you don't mind," Jenny said, "I'd like to hear *exactly* what happened outside. If some creep is hanging around the club scaring people, Dad and I need to know about it, so we can get rid of him."

Karen squirmed. "I told you, it was probably my imagination. I just thought I heard a noise."

Jenny looked at her keenly, and Karen noticed how big and bright her violet eyes were. Those eyes can see *through* me, the teenager thought. She knows I'm lying. But of course, that was silly. She was still so shaken that her mind was playing tricks on her.

Jenny said, "I can't help feeling something's wrong in your life. If so, it might help to talk about it." She smiled. "People are supposed to confide in their bartenders."

Karen shook her head. "Look, I admit, I'm having a problem, but not one anybody else would understand."

"You mean, I wouldn't believe you," Jenny said. "But I might. I have a special . . . talent with 'hunches,' you might say. I have a 'hunch' that you aren't crazy or a practical joker, and my 'hunches' are usually right. That's what brought me outside just now. I felt that someone was in trouble, and lo and behold, there you were."

"All right, I will tell," Karen said. "On one condition: it stays between you and me. No matter what you think, you can't call my parents, my school, or anybody."

"Deal," Jenny said. Karen told her all that had happened.

By the time she finished, Jenny was scowling. "This is monstrous," she said.

Karen said, "Then . . . you do believe me?"

"Yes," Jenny said. "And I'm not going to let this atrocity happen. I — "

"Yes, you are," a male voice said.

Startled, Karen lurched around, nearly knocking over her Coke. The old man, Jenny's father, was standing behind her.

Jenny said, "Dad, if you overheard, then you know this girl and her boyfriend are in danger."

"It's not our problem. Our problem is to obey the compact. We are not to interfere."

Jenny glared at Mr. Demos for a moment, then

101

dropped her eyes. "I know," Jenny sighed.

Karen could see that Jenny wanted to help her, but now, it was plain, she wouldn't. Karen nearly started to cry. It felt awful to gain an ally, then have her snatched away.

"Well, at least I can advise her," Jenny said. "There's no rule against that."

"That's debatable," Mr. Demos said. "But if you must, tell her to stay out of it. If you encourage her to fight a ghost, her blood will be on your hands."

Karen realized they were talking about her as if she weren't there, just as the adults in the nurse's office had. Suddenly, she was angry. *"You* stay out of *this,"* she said to the white-haired man. "What do you care what happens to me anyway?"

Mr. Demos's lip curled. Karen couldn't tell whether it was in amusement or contempt. "I don't," he said. He looked back at Jenny. "So help her throw her life away. Why not?" He turned and strode away.

"I'm sorry about that," Jenny said. "He—"

"He believed me about Joy," Karen said. "Just like you did. Why, when nobody else would? Who are you people *really?* Not *just* a father and daughter who run a teen club, I can tell that."

"People who sometimes see what others can't," Jenny replied. "I'm sorry, I can't say more than that. But surely the important thing is not what I am, but whether I can help you."

"All right," Karen said. She wished Jenny would reveal more, but at least she sensed that the ash-blond woman truly was on her side. "What can you tell me about Joy?"

"I don't know anything about her specifically, but I do know about ghosts in general, and that information may help you. Knowledge is power."

"Okay, then tell me this: how come Mike and I are the only ones who can see Joy?"

"Mike can see her because she wants him to," Jenny said. "As for you, well, I think it's because you care so much about him. Sometimes love is power, too. In this case, the power to pierce your enemy's invisibility."

Love? Karen felt herself blush. "Why is Joy bothering Mike?"

Jenny sipped her Coke. "It's hard to say, because ghosts are usually insane. If they weren't, they'd move on to the next world. And because they're human souls, with motives as diverse as those of the living. My guess is that Mike reminds her of someone she hated when she was alive. She missed getting revenge on that person, and destroying a substitute seems like the next best thing."

"She was killed by a drunk driver!" Karen said. "That has to be it."

Jenny said, "Maybe. It fits."

"But why is she hurting him in such a complicated way?" Karen asked. "Why doesn't she just stick a knife in him?"

Jenny shrugged. "Once again, it's anybody's guess. I suspect it's a game to her. Making Mike drink and drive is more satisfying. More fun. Destroying him this way will last longer."

"But she could hurt a person another way if she wanted to, couldn't she?" Karen asked, trembling. "She could stick a knife in me."

"Yes," Jenny said. "But don't despair. She isn't all-powerful. She probably can't swing a weapon so hard and fast that no one could get out of the way. And she can't attack you nonstop. Everything she does drains her strength, and eventually she has to rest. That may be why she tried to scare you off before. For most ghosts, making illusions is less tiring than moving real objects around."

For a moment, Karen felt a little better. Then a thought struck her. "But what if she comes after me when I'm asleep? Locked doors won't keep her out, will they?"

Jenny said, "Probably not. So let's hope you can get rid of her quickly."

"How?" Karen asked. "How do I do that?"

"Many ghosts are bound to something. Often, it's their remains, occasionally, some possession. Whatever it is, it anchors them to the earth.

"If the anchor is what's left of Joy's body, you'll know when you look at her grave. The power buried there will poison the ground for several yards around, blighting the vegetation and crumbling the tombstones.

"If the anchor's a treasured personal item, you may well see a duplicate of it in the image Joy presents to you. Perhaps it's a piece of jewelry, or an article of clothing.

"Whatever it is, destroying it should send Joy on to the next world."

"But I don't know anything about Joy's life," Karen said. "How am I supposed to find her anchor?"

"I guess you'll have to play detective," Jenny said. "Do you have any more questions?" Karen shook her head. "Then finish your drink, and I'll drive you home. I doubt you want to walk through the woods again."

Eighteen

Karen made it back up the elm and in her window without getting caught. Then she lay in bed staring, waiting for Joy's white face to loom out of the shadows. Finally, an hour before Sunday morning's sunrise, she dropped into a fitful, nightmare-haunted doze.

She awoke Sunday morning at eight, sweaty and trembling, feeling as if she hadn't slept at all. Still, the sunlight streaming in the window was reassuring, even though Joy could appear by day as easily as night. The sizzle and scent of frying bacon was coming up the stairs. Maybe breakfast would help her feel less groggy.

By the time she made it to the kitchen table, Mom, Dad, and Paula were close to finishing their meals. "Good morning," Mom said. "My goodness, your eyes are red! Didn't you sleep? Do you feel all right?"

"If you were lying awake, I hope it was because you were thinking about your prank," Dad said. Obviously, he wasn't ready to let Karen off the hook.

"I was," Karen said, doing her best to sound remorseful, "and I really am sorry. Look, I know I'm grounded, but may I go to the library after church? I have to research a paper for World History."

"I bet you really want to go see Mike," Paula said.

Karen could have smacked her.

Dad frowned. "I was thinking you should clean the house today. As part of your punishment."

For a moment, Karen was afraid she was trapped. Then Mom said, "I just did clean. And Karen has to do her schoolwork."

"All right, go," Dad growled. "But make sure you come straight home after you finish."

"Yes, sir," Karen said meekly.

After breakfast and church, Karen changed from her dress to jeans, grabbed her jacket, pencils, and a spiral notebook, then set off down the street.

The air was pleasantly crisp. The sky was blue with wisps of white cloud, and the leaves still clinging to the trees were red and gold. In other circumstances, she would have enjoyed such a lovely morning, but now she was too busy watching for her enemy.

The Cooper Hollow Library stood at the corner of Main and Albany, catty-corner from City Hall. Both buildings were big and gray, with rows of round pillars in front. A bronze statue of Jeremiah Cooper, musket in hand, guarded the approach to City Hall, while a pair of stone lions flanked the stairs leading up to the library.

As Karen neared the library, she studied the cars and other people on the street. For one heart-stopping moment, she thought she saw Mike's car, then realized she was looking at a different red Mustang, with a brighter finish, and no rust spots.

The teenager hurried into the library, then peered about again. The place wasn't busy. In fact, as far as she could tell, she was the first patron to arrive. If Joy found her here, there might not be any witnesses around to save her.

But Joy *isn't* here, Karen thought. So stop scaring yourself and get on with what you have to do.

She wondered where she should start looking. Well,

she assumed that Joy had died in Cooper Hollow, and the library had books about local history on the third floor.

Karen climbed the slippery marble stairs. Her steps echoed hollowly.

When she reached the third floor, she saw that the information desk was vacant. A sign on it read, ASSISTANCE AVAILABLE AT MAIN DESK. Swallowing, she walked on toward the stacks.

Moving between the bookshelves was like stepping into a cave. In the center of the room, where the tables, chairs, and card files sat, fluorescent lights shone, and sunbeams poured through the skylights, but little of that illumination reached her. The narrow aisles were so gloomy that she had to lean close to the books to read the faded writing on their spines. Floating dust tickled her nose. The odor of decaying paper hung in the air.

Trying once again not to feel nervous, she pulled out a book about the Hollow. As far as she could tell from the table of contents, it didn't contain a list of residents, nor was Joyce Carrier's name in the index. She exchanged the volume for another. The new one didn't have a table of contents or index. Karen frowned, realizing what a long search this could turn out to be.

Beyond the stacks, in the open part of the room, footsteps brushed the carpet.

Karen shuddered. Told herself, it isn't Joy. But she had to be sure. She tiptoed to the end of the bookshelf and peeked around it.

She didn't see anyone. Perhaps she'd only imagined the sound. Or perhaps Joy was already hidden from view, stalking through the stacks, hunting her.

But Karen couldn't drop everything and run, just because the ghost *might* be near. If she fled every time she heard a noise, or glimpsed a shadow from the corner of her eye, she'd never accomplish anything. So

107

she scowled and returned to the books.

The library grew darker, making it even harder to read the print on the musty, brown-edged pages. She told herself the sun must have gone behind a cloud.

Then the book in her hands, a huge tome about Cooper Hollow during the Depression, made a squelching sound, and quivered. A mass of squirming gray worms chewed their way out of the pages.

Karen yelped and threw the book down. It banged on the floor. The worms, and the holes they'd gnawed, faded into nothingness.

Oh no! Karen thought. The worms weren't real! Joy made me see them, to get me to yell, and now she knows where I am!

Karen had to move before Joy got to her. Her first impulse was to run toward the stairs. If she could get to where there were other people, she'd be safe. But the ghost was probably staying toward the center of the room, ready to attack her. So Karen darted to the far end of the stacks, then edged along between the shelves and the wall.

She heard a footfall in the aisle she'd just vacated. "K — a — a — r — e — n!" Joy called. Her voice echoed through the cavernous room. It was almost impossible to believe the librarians on the first floor couldn't hear it.

I could scream, Karen thought. They'd hear *me*. But the sound would lead Joy to her first.

The teenager decided that if she tried to hide in one place, Joy would find her. If she kept moving silently, maybe she could stay ahead of the ghost until someone else came upstairs. Struggling to breathe quietly, she sidled on.

"You threw down a book," Joy said. "You tore the binding. The librarian's going to be mad at you." She giggled.

Karen tried to judge Joy's location from her voice.

But the sound came from one part of the room, then, instantly, another. Once, it seemed to originate next to the live girl's ear, startling her badly. As she sucked in a breath to scream, she realized that Joy wasn't really beside her, but she felt as if she had to shriek anyway. She jammed her knuckle in her mouth and bit down hard. The stab of pain pushed her panic away.

"I know Demos and his daughter refused to help you," Joy said. "That should have convinced you to give up. Remember, I can feel you with my mind. You can't *study* me, not here, at City Hall, or the *Gazette* either. As soon as you try, I'll know."

Karen reached the corner of the room, then crept on down the next wall. She kept peering between the shelves, but still couldn't see Joy. She supposed that was good, if it meant the spirit couldn't see her either.

"It isn't too late to make friends," Joy said. "Just come out and talk. Just give me your word you'll leave Mike and me alone. If you don't, I'm afraid that Karen Bradley, that poor girl who's been acting so strangely at school, is going to commit suicide. Maybe by jumping off the roof."

Karen turned another corner. Now, at last, she caught a glimpse of Joy. The ghost had her back turned. She was still checking the stacks on the other side of the room. In fact, she was slinking toward the far wall. Evidently she'd decided that was the only way to make sure Karen wasn't cowering motionless behind the end of a shelf.

By leaving the center of the room, Joy had given Karen a chance to reach the stairs. Karen took a deep breath, then crept down the aisle between two bookshelves. The ghost began to turn. It was too late to duck back out of sight, so Karen started running. Her footsteps pounded.

Joy disappeared. Karen heard a rhythmic thump-thump-thump. But it wasn't until the bookshelf on her left toppled that she grasped what had happened.

The Joy she'd seen had been an illusion, devised to flush her out. The real Joy was standing at the end of Karen's row of stacks. When she'd heard Karen running, she'd shoved the nearest shelf. It had fallen into the one beside it, that one into the next, and now the whole formation was crashing down like a chain of dominoes.

Karen tried to scramble clear. She was too slow. A wave of books hammered down on her, followed by the heavy bookshelf itself an instant later.

The next thing she knew, she was lying in darkness, a crushing, suffocating weight on top of her. For a minute, she couldn't remember what had happened. Then a sneering white face flashed into her mind.

Joy! Joy had buried her and was no doubt striding toward her right now!

She tried to heave herself up. The mass on top of her held her down. Straining, sobbing, she thrashed. This time, she felt the objects atop her shift. Her head and shoulders burst into the light, jammed through the center of a bookshelf.

To Karen's surprise, Joy was still a few yards away. Evidently the ghost hadn't been able to tell where, in the chaos of fallen furniture and scattered books, Karen was trapped. But now Joy came flickering toward her, her red-nailed hands outstretched.

Karen fought to drag her lower body free, but her hips caught. Joy leaned over her.

The teenager grabbed a book and swung it, thinking, this won't help, you can't hit a ghost! But the volume whacked Joy's face. The pale girl stumbled back. Books slid beneath her foot, spilling her to the floor.

Once again, Karen tried to wrench herself free. Her hips popped loose. Writhing, she dragged her legs clear of the shelving. Books cascaded away from her kicking feet.

110

Joy rolled to her knees, then lunged at her. Karen threw herself sideways, then leaped up and raced for the stairs. She started down, but her foot skidded on the marble. Suddenly the stairwell yawned like a deep white pit. If she ran down, she could fall and break her neck. But there was no choice. Joy's footsteps were pattering behind her.

She hurtled on, praying she'd meet a librarian coming up. Surely someone had heard the shelves crash down. But of course, they'd only fallen a few moments ago.

Second floor landing. No one in sight. She swung herself around the bend in the staircase and ran on.

A brown-haired woman with glasses hanging on a chain around her neck appeared at the foot of the steps. When she saw Karen running down at her, her mouth fell open.

A witness! Karen thought. I'm safe! Then hands thumped her back. Hurled forward into space, Karen realized that Joy had pushed her from behind without worrying about spectators. The fall would look like an accident.

Nineteen

Karen bounced down the steps, striking one after another. The world spun. A final tumble left her sprawled on her back, arms outstretched.

For a moment, she was dazed. Then she gasped in a breath and jackknifed up.

There was no one on the steps, no one beside her except the librarian. For the moment, at least, Joy was gone.

"Don't try to move!" the brown-haired woman squawked. "You could be injured!" She grabbed Karen's shoulders and slammed her back down on the floor.

Karen wondered how badly she was hurt. She could see and hear okay, she wasn't bleeding, and her arms and legs worked. As far as she could tell, she was basically okay. Maybe the carpet at the bottom of the stairs had cushioned the last impact.

She started to sit up again, and the librarian shoved her back. Jeez, Karen thought, I survived the fall, but this woman might kill me. "I'm all right," she said.

The librarian raised her hand. "How many fingers am I holding up?"

"Two," Karen said.

"Where does it hurt?"

"All over," the teenager said. "But none of it's bad. I'm okay. Really. I just need to catch my breath."

The woman eyed her doubtfully. "Well. All right. What made all the noise up there? Why were you running?"

Karen sighed. She was tired of lying, but there was no real choice. "Some shelves fell. I don't know why. I thought I should tell someone fast, so I was hurrying."

The librarian frowned. "The shelves just fell of their own accord? That doesn't make sense. What's your name?"

Karen stood up, wincing at the twinges the motion produced. "I have to go."

The brown-haired woman hastily jumped up, too. "No, you can't, not yet."

Karen didn't want to stay here. Joy might still be lurking about. Nor did she want the librarian to find out who she was, and get her in more trouble with her parents. She tried to sound like some stuck-up rich girl from the Riding Academy. "You can't keep me here. My daddy's a lawyer, so I know. If you mess with me, we'll sue the town for having an unsafe staircase."

The librarian glared. "All right, go." Karen scurried out the door.

She walked aimlessly down the street, keeping an eye out for Joy, limping slightly when her left leg began to ache worse than her right. She wondered what to do next.

To get rid of Joy, she had to learn about the ghost girl's mortal life. But if she tried, Joy would prevent it. It seemed like a puzzle without an answer.

But did Joy know every move Karen made? If so, then Karen had no chance. She had to hope that the phantom could sense some of her actions, but not all.

Maybe Joy had her psychic awareness targeted on particular locations. But if Karen could think of somewhere else to look for information, a place Joy hadn't considered, she might be able to go there safely. But where would that place be?

When the answer occurred to her, she grinned. Suddenly oblivious to her aches and pains, she started jogging.

Fifteen minutes later, she reached Joan's beige, two-story house. She glanced around, making sure there was no sign of Joy, then trotted up to the door and rang the bell.

Joan answered it. "Hey," she said, "the madwoman of Cooper High. I'm stunned to see you. I thought your folks would ground you for life. What made you pull such a dumb stunt?"

Karen shrugged. "It seemed funny at the time. Can I come in? I need a favor."

"Sure. *Mi casa es tu casa.*" She ushered her in, then led her to her bedroom.

Karen had always thought Joan's room displayed a sort of split personality. Posters of Axel Rose, Christian Slater, and Jason Priestly shared the space with a periodic table of the elements, a bookshelf crammed with math and science texts and issues of *Scientific American,* and an Amiga computer. The tall girl flopped down on the chair in front of the machine. "What's up?" she asked.

Karen sat on the unmade waterbed. It bounced beneath her. "You once told me a person can find out all kinds of things with a computer. Over the phone."

Joan eyed her warily. "Right. Your computer can talk to somebody else's."

"You also said you'd hacked into some systems where you didn't have any business. Just to see if you could do it."

"Well, yeah. So?"

Karen took a deep breath. "Can you get into the city records?"

Joan nodded.

"Well, I need to find out about a girl named Joyce

114

Carrier," Karen continued. "I think she lived around here, and I'm almost positive she died here, in an accident with a drunk driver."

"What else do you know about her?"

"Nothing."

The tall girl raised her eyebrows. "So why do you *want* to know about her?"

Karen groped for another lie, then decided, the heck with it. She shouldn't lie to a friend. "I can't explain. You just have to trust me that it's important."

Joan frowned. "I liked you better when you weren't so secretive. But all right. Let's see what we can dig up." She switched on the Amiga, then loaded a disk. The computer hummed and clicked. She rose, opened the door, and yelled, "I'm on the modem. Don't pick up the phone."

"All right!" her father answered from elsewhere in the house.

Joan sat back down, grinned, and cracked her knuckles. "Now you'll see the master at work," she said.

Karen tried to smile back, but she was too jittery to share her friend's high spirits. It had seemed to her that there was something old-fashioned about Joy's dress and hairstyle. That might mean the pale girl had died before the computer age, and so didn't understand that someone could examine the town records by remote control. If so, she might not sense what Karen was attempting.

But Karen was only guessing. The ghost could appear in the bedroom any second. She swallowed away the dryness in her mouth and tried not to shiver.

"I'm in," Joan said. "I'll bring up the death data." She tapped keys. New yellow characters appeared on the black screen.

"Did you find her?" Karen asked.

"Not yet," Joan said. "Chill. Cripes, what idiot

115

wrote this program? The way the data is filed, this is going to take forever. Unless you can give me something more to go on."

Karen visualized Joy. Suddenly she realized the ghost was wearing a *flapper* dress. But could she have lived *that* long ago? Well, why not? Time probably didn't mean much to spirits, and no doubt there'd been drunk drivers in the Prohibition era, too. "Check the records from the 1920s," she said.

"Why didn't you say so before?" asked Joan. She typed in a command. The screen flickered. "Bingo! Joyce Alice Carrier, born August 3, 1908, died November 11, 1924. Father, Howard Carrier, mother, Alice Morris Carrier, residence, 509 Cross Road."

"What else have you got?" Karen asked.

"Let's check the property records." The computer keys clicked. "The last owner and occupant of the house was Edwina Carrier, Joyce's younger sister," Joan said at last. "She never married and has no children. She also died last month, without leaving a will. Since there are no Carriers left, the house is going to the state."

"What else can you get?" Karen asked.

Joan snorted. "Are you kidding? Nothing. You're darn lucky somebody bothered to enter this much, considering how old some of the data is."

Frustrated, Karen raked her fingers through her coppery hair. She knew a lot more than she had a minute ago, but still not enough. Of course, now that she knew when Joy lived, it should be easy to find out more. Except that if she went back to the library, the ghost would sense it.

Maybe *Joan* could do the research without getting caught. But Karen had endangered her too much already. How could she possibly ask her?

With Mike's life and her own in *certain* danger, how could she not?

"You're looking at me really weird," the tall girl said. "What is it?"

"I need you to do something else for me," Karen said. "Go to the library and find out everything you can about Joyce. Check the microfiche copies of the Cooper *Gazette* and anything else you can think of." She remembered what Jenny had told her, that many ghosts were anchored by their earthly remains. "I particularly need to know where she's buried."

"You've got to be kidding," Joan said. "What the *heck*—no, never mind, you won't tell me. Or why you can't go to the library for yourself either, I suppose. All right, but you owe me."

"That's right," Karen said, "I do." She blinked back a tear.

Joan gaped at her. "Well, good grief, don't get all sloppy about it. You can wait here if you want. My folks won't care." She imitated Arnold Schwarzenegger: "I'll be back." She grabbed her jacket from the closet, her purse and a yellow legal pad from her desk, and disappeared down the hall. The house's front door thumped shut a moment later.

Afterward, Karen had nothing to do but wait. One hour passed. Two. Three.

By the end of the fourth, she was almost frantic. Why hadn't she warned Joan that something might try to hurt her?

I have to go find her, Karen thought, jumping up from her seat. Maybe it isn't too late, maybe—

The bedroom door opened, startling her. She stumbled back against the waterbed.

Joan stepped into the room. "Whoa," she said. "What's the matter?"

Karen realized she must look terrified. She tried to smile. "Nothing. I didn't hear the front door. You surprised me."

"Well, switch to decaf. I got your data."

Karen swallowed. "Did anything . . . funny happen?"

"Not to me, but *somebody* tore up the third floor of the library this morning. I had to pout and plead to be allowed up there. One of the librarians asked me if I knew the girl who did the damage. I said her description sounded like a redhead who goes to Cooper Riding."

Karen blushed. "Thank you."

"Are you *sure* you don't want to tell me what's going on? Maybe I could help you more."

Karen was tempted. But she knew that even if Joan believed her, she'd be no protection against an attacker she couldn't see. "If I *could* explain, I swear I would."

Joan sighed. "All right, be that way. Here's what I found out. Your friend Joy—that's what everybody called her—was a rich kid and a troublemaker. A rebel. She liked to drink, ride in fast cars, and party. In those days, the best place to have her kind of fun was a speakeasy in the woods." She paused. "Do you know what that was?"

Karen grimaced. "A club where people drank when drinking was illegal. I took American History, too, remember?"

"Just making sure you're with me. Anyway, I think the speakeasy was in the same building where the Nightmare Club is now. Joy snuck out there a lot. I guess it didn't bother her or anybody else who hung out there that she was still a kid.

"Eventually she started dating a guy named Frank Yazel. They were two of a kind. Frank made his living driving whiskey in from Canada. He had to drive fast to dodge the police, and he liked to drive fast for fun, too. To race. One night at the speakeasy, he got drunk, then he and another man decided to race from the club to Cross Road.

"Wild as Joy was, even she could tell Frank was too

loaded to race, particularly on such a narrow, twisting road. She tried to talk him out of it, and when she couldn't, she tried to stay behind.

"It made Frank mad. He punched her, and witnesses heard him threaten to break every bone in her body if she didn't ride with him as usual. And so, sobbing, she climbed in the car.

"She should have let him beat her. He lost control on one of the curves. His car plowed into a tree, and they both got killed. Joy flew through the windshield head-first. It sort of—"

"Tore her face in half," Karen said.

"Yeah," Joan said. "Her parents had a closed-coffin funeral. How did you know? If you already had this data, why did I have to spend hours—"

"I promise, I didn't," Karen said. "I truly did need you to get it. Did you learn where Joy is buried?"

The tall girl nodded. "Riverside Cemetery. The *Gazette* had photos of the burial, and I tried to figure out the grave's exact location from them. You know that monument—the one that Oswald Cooper's widow erected for him? It's a statue of a kneeling angel praying?"

Karen nodded.

"Well, as near as I could make out, Joy's is about fifty yards east of it, on a piece of ground that sticks out in the water. Her marker's a Calvary cross, a cross on a three-step pyramid, and she's planted with a bunch of other Carriers."

"Thank you," Karen said. "This is exactly what I needed."

"Good," Joan said. "I just wish I knew what you're going to do with it."

There was only one thing to do. Go look at the grave and see if the area was blighted. If so, Karen would have to dig up and destroy whatever was left of Joy's body.

She cringed from the thought of doing it in the dark, alone. But if she tried in the daylight, someone would see, and stop her. And even Joan would refuse to help her do something so apparently crazy, beside which, she'd endangered her friend too much already.

She glanced out the window and was dismayed to see how quickly the sun was falling down the western sky. She had to hurry if she was going to get to the cemetery before nightfall.

Twenty

Mike tilted his head back, and gin burned down his throat. It tasted so good that for a moment, he was tempted to keep gulping till the flask was empty. But of course he didn't want to look like a pig. Reluctantly, he passed the bottle back.

As Joy took it, her dark eyes narrowed. "Turn the car around," she said.

Mike blinked. *"Again?"*

"Yes."

"More private business?"

She nodded. "This time, I'm going to finish it."

He felt a flash of anger. He couldn't help thinking how Pete and Dave would laugh if they saw him jumping to obey Joy's every order without even understanding what was going on. They'd say he was whipped *bad.* "No way. At least not till you tell me what it is."

"Just trust me, it's important."

"Trust *me,* and explain."

Joy sneered. "I thought we could have some real fun together. But right now, you're starting to bore me. If you don't know how to be nice, maybe it's time to finish this."

"You mean you want to dump me?"

"You could put it that way. Dump you down a cold, dark hole, where there's no booze and no me."

He almost told her to go ahead. Then a wave of

panic washed away his anger. His life would be cold and dark without her. She was the only one who liked or understood him. The only person who was any fun.

"I'm sorry!" he said, swinging the Mustang into a U turn. The tires squealed. "I'll do what you want. Just don't leave me!"

"I won't," she said. "Not if you're ready to be your old, sweet self again." She handed him the flask. "Here, let's drink to making up."

Karen arrived at Riverside Cemetery at dusk. The graveyard was one of the oldest in the Hollow. The white forms of saints, soldiers, crosses, and miniature palaces—all ornate monuments favored by by-gone generations of mourners—floated in the gloom, and glowed in the twilight. Nearby, the gray expanse of the river glimmered.

The cemetery was too far from Karen's house to walk, so she'd ridden her bike, with Mom's gardening shovel tied to the handlebars. She dismounted, then looked around to see if anyone was near. As far as she could tell, she was alone.

After leaving Joan's house, she'd gone home to collect the tools she thought she might need: the spade, to open the grave; a short crowbar, suitable for prying the lids off coffins; Dad's heavyweight Kabar survival knife, for self-defense; and a flashlight. While there, it had occurred to her that she'd better phone Jenny, to ask how to be sure she was really "destroying" an anchor. After all, time might have damaged a seventy year-old corpse pretty thoroughly already. The ash-blond woman had recommended fire. Supposedly, its purifying energy transformed matter in the most fundamental way possible. So Karen had added a bottle of lighter fluid and a book of matches to her arsenal.

Unfortunately, her preparations had taken longer

than expected, and thus she'd reached the graveyard later than she wished. But there's still time, she told herself nervously. I can get in, check the grave, and be back out before dark.

Unless, of course, it turned out that Joy's remains were the anchor. Then Karen would have to stay past nightfall, and dig. It was hard to hope that things would turn out that way, even though it would mean that she was close to the solution to her problem.

She started to lift her bike over the knee-high granite wall, then hesitated. What if Joy had her awareness focused on the graveyard, too?

The answer was, it didn't matter. Karen had to try to save Mike no matter what. Frowning, she set her bike on the other side of the barrier, then climbed over herself.

She freed the spade, then laid it and the bike on the ground, so no one passing on the road would see them. Crouching, she crept east, toward the river. The shadows seemed to lengthen with every step she took.

The air in the cemetery seemed colder than that outside. Shivering, she told herself it was just her imagination. Often, she stumbled, tripping over the mounds of new graves, or stepping in the hollows created by the collapse of old ones. The jolts made her bruises ache. Once she skulked past the debris of a recent funeral, and smelled the sickly bouquet of the rotting lilies.

Repeatedly, she glimpsed pale figures from the corner of her eye. Then, gasping, she whirled, only to find that she hadn't seen Joy but one of the blank-eyed statues.

She'd entered the cemetery due west of where she judged Oswald Cooper's monument should be, and soon, the kneeling angel loomed out of the murk. She smiled to see that she'd reckoned correctly.

As she passed the winged figure, a chill oozed up her spine. Suddenly she was certain it had turned its head to watch her. She lurched around. The angel looked no different than before. She swallowed and prowled on.

She tried to pace off fifty yards, and found herself by the riverbank, close enough to hear the murmur of the current. She read the names on tombstones. Carl. Kropp. Bujold.

Obviously, she was in the wrong place. Unfortunately, there was no way to know whether she'd veered too far north or south, or blundered right past Joy's grave. She started working her way back toward the praying angel, zigzagging, seeking a Calvary cross, or a stone reading Carrier.

Meanwhile, the air darkened like clotting blood, until it became difficult to make out the carving on the markers. She wished she hadn't left the flashlight in her bicycle basket, but who would have guessed this would take so *long!* Maddeningly, Calvary crosses sprang up like toadstools, and she had to go and peer at every one.

A few minutes later, she arrived at the kneeling statue. Doggedly, Karen turned and trudged back toward the river, this time swinging farther north. Finally, as the last bit of gray light died in the west, she stumbled across a marker that read, ALICE MORRIS CARRIER, BELOVED MOTHER, SEPT. 19, 1887 TO JAN. 5, 1943.

Karen found Joy's grave to the right of her mother's, then peered about. Jenny had said that the area surrounding the grave would be blighted if the body was the anchor. As far as she could tell, the grass and bushes were flourishing here just as well as they were elsewhere in the cemetery. And the tombstones weren't decaying any faster. Evidently, Joy's body wasn't the anchor. Karen felt a guilty pang of relief that she wouldn't have to dig it up. She turned to go.

Out on the highway, a car motor hummed. Twin headlights stabbed through the wrought-iron cemetery gate. Metal clanked, hinges squealed, a door thumped, and the automobile rolled into the cemetery.

It was either Joy, Karen figured, or it was the police, patrolling to catch trespassers.

Well, whoever it was, she didn't want to get caught. She crouched down behind a rectangular marker.

She wished the car would turn. There were lots of narrow dirt lanes in the graveyard. But the intruder kept heading straight for her. Finally it was close enough for her to make out the distinctive shape of an old Mustang.

And Joy must be inside! Karen whimpered. Her heart pounded. She fought an impulse to curl into a ball.

The Mustang's lights swept over her hiding place. The car stopped. "I see you," Joy called.

It was obvious from the aim of the headlights that she did. So I won't cower like a scared rabbit, Karen thought. Somehow, she made herself rise, then stood blinking in the glare.

Beyond the light, in the Mustang's front seats, sat two figures. Joy was beside the wheel. Mike slumped beside her, his head lolling.

Karen couldn't believe her friend would let Joy hurt her if he understood what was going on. "Mike!" she screamed. "Wake up!"

Mike raised his head and peered about. His dull eyes gazed at Karen without a flicker of recognition, and then he turned to Joy. She handed him the silver flask. He threw back his head and guzzled. Clear liquor ran out the corner of his mouth. His Adam's apple bobbed.

"He won't help you," Joy said. "He's too far gone to grasp what's happening. This time, there's nobody to help you."

"You don't have to kill me," Karen said. "Obviously, I came to the graveyard because I thought your anchor was here. Since I don't know where it really is, there's nothing I can do to you."

Joy laughed. "Nice try. But you couldn't have learned where I was buried without discovering other things, too. And that makes you dangerous."

She realizes I must also know where she lived, Karen thought. And if she's worried about it, the anchor must be there! "It's crazy for you to hurt me, or Mike either. He isn't Frank Yazel. He's nothing like Frank Yazel. He isn't a criminal, and he'd never hurt anybody. He wouldn't be drinking the way he is if you weren't forcing him."

Joy said, "You don't know him as well as you think you do. But anyway, he's enough like Frank to make him fun to kill."

Karen glanced at Mike. Hear this, she pleaded silently. Understand what she's saying. But the boy was slumping again, dazed or passed out.

Karen stared into Joy's dark eyes. "I beg you," she said, "let us go. Your death was sad and unfair— "

" 'Sad and unfair,' " Joy mimicked. "You don't know what those words mean." Her voice quavered, as if she was about to sob. "I was so young. There were so many things I wanted to do. Mama and Papa were going to take me to Europe!"

"You're right," Karen said. "I can't really know how terrible it was. But I do know it doesn't give you the right to take out your anger on innocent people. Heck, it was partly your own fault! You set yourself up to get hurt!"

Joy glared, then said, "Even if I hadn't wanted to kill you before, I would now." Tires squealing, the Mustang shot forward.

Karen wheeled and ran. There's a way out of this, she told herself desperately. I just have to find it.

Headlights speared her body. She heard the Mustang hurtling up behind her. She threw herself sideways, slipped, fell to one knee behind a stubby brown

126

tombstone. She knew without looking that she hadn't timed her move properly. The Mustang was about to swerve and run her down.

It didn't. It shot past ten feet to her left, braked, and began to turn around.

Peering about, Karen realized that she'd landed in a cluster of markers. In the darkness, the cemetery looked like an open field, but it wasn't, and a car couldn't maneuver among the tombstones and statues as easily as a person on foot. Since Joy could run faster than her quarry, she could probably murder her more easily if she left the car. But maybe she was having fun, making a game of it.

Unfortunately, Karen couldn't simply hunker down somewhere the Mustang couldn't reach. Joy would get out of the vehicle then. The live girl had to keep moving.

So she dashed down a row of veterans' star markers sticking up from the ground like daisies. Her pursuer roared after her. The headlights caught her. She dodged right, past a stone shaft.

For the moment, she was keeping away from the Mustang pretty well. But it was only a matter of time until her legs gave out, or she zigged instead of zagged, and then Joy would nail her. She couldn't just run in circles, she had to get out of the cemetery.

There were two ways out, go back the way she came or leap into the river. She thought she was still closer to the river, and she'd once seen a movie where someone claimed that evil spirits couldn't cross running water, so she decided to take that route.

She peered about to get her bearings, then gasped.

The granite wall was gone. The river ringed the cemetery like a moat around a castle. Four pairs of headlights circled her.

It's just illusion, Karen thought. I can't let it throw me. I still see Oswald Cooper's angel, so I can use it to navigate to the real river. But how could she avoid four cars? While she was dodging the fake ones, the real one could catch her from behind.

She didn't know, but she had to try. She sprinted in what she prayed was the right direction, weaving back and forth, darting through thick clusters of markers whenever possible.

Despite her attempts at evasion, one of the cars was poised to attack when she reached the next dirt lane. She raced forward. The Mustang roared at her, missed by inches. The wind of its passage almost knocked her down.

She staggered on, spent a precious second glancing back to make sure that the praying angel was still where it was supposed to be, still facing the way it was supposed to face. Another Mustang lunged at her. She threw herself out of its path, then noticed that its tires were passing through gravestones without crushing them. It was a mirage.

Which meant that it had been faking her out, setting her up for a real attack. She whirled, and another Mustang charged. She leaped to one side. Brakes squealing, the car careened past her and slammed into a mausoleum. Metal crunched, glass shattered, and one headlight went out. For a heartbeat, Karen dared to hope that now she'd be able to tell the real Mustang from the fake ones, but then each of the phonies lost a light, too. The damaged vehicle backed away from the tomb.

Karen ran. Headlights circled like sharks. She scrambled past a standing angel, this one with graffiti spray-painted on its robe and half its head broken off. Suddenly she was in an open area, with cars about to charge her from three sides. Joy's face leered from behind each steering wheel.

Karen knew she'd never avoid all the cars. She had perhaps three seconds to pick out the real Mustang from the fakes, or she was as good as dead. She peered wildly about. Some instinct prompted her to bite her knuckle, as she had in the library, so she did.

The jab of pain quieted the terror shrieking through her mind, helped her focus her concentration. Suddenly, she thought she *could* tell which cars were illusions. For an instant, the one on her left seemed transparent, like mist, and the growl of the one in front of her seemed to fade.

The three cars raced at her. Knowing that Joy would swerve to follow if she moved too soon, she held herself motionless for another instant. Then she darted straight at the Mustang on the left.

The car hurtled to meet her, now looking as solid as rock. Suddenly certain that she'd guessed wrong, she cringed. The Mustang struck her and swept on without hurting her. She didn't even feel the blow.

She grinned savagely, and ran on, still trying to spot which cars were mirages. When one wavered or fell silent, she knew to ignore it and dodge the others.

Ahead, the river suddenly shimmered into view, less than fifty feet away. She sprinted by a stone urn full of dead roses, then scrambled behind an oak to evade one of the Mustangs.

She looked up to see only taillights. All four cars had made their passes, and now needed to turn before they could charge again. If Karen could make it into the water in the next few seconds, Joy wouldn't get another chance to run her over.

Karen sprinted. But when she reached the top of the steep bank, she slipped on the grass and fell to her hands and knees.

Suddenly, a black mass roared out of the shadows. Horrified, Karen realized that, for the last few seconds at least, all four of the cars she'd been dodging had been illusions. The real Mustang had been lurking there, its lights extinguished.

129

She scrambled to her feet, knowing she was moving too slowly. This time, Joy was going to hit her. But something amazing happened first. Mike. Behind the windshield, Mike raised his head. Seeing Karen in danger, he jerked around and yanked the steering wheel.

Too late. The Mustang still struck Karen. She tumbled through the air, fell toward the water, and then the world went black.

Twenty-one

Joy shoved Mike, tearing his hands off the steering wheel. She stomped on the brake. Squealing, the Mustang lurched to a stop at the edge of the drop.

The pale girl jumped out and peered at the river. Confused and frightened, Mike climbed out and ran up beside her. What was happening? Surely the jumbled images in his mind were only the residue of some nightmare. Surely they hadn't just run Karen down.

"What did we hit?" he asked.

"Just then?" she asked, still gazing at the river. "Nothing, no thanks to you. The way you snatched at the wheel, I think you were having a bad dream."

"If we didn't run into anything, why are you looking at the water?"

"Because you scared me, and it's helping calm me down." Smiling, she finally turned to face him. "What did you dream, anyway? What did you *think* happened?"

Mike swallowed. "I thought you ran over Karen Bradley."

Joy giggled. "What would be the point of that, since I already took you away from her?"

"Don't laugh! I swear, I *saw* it!"

The dark-haired girl pouted. "Let me get this straight. Are you truly *accusing* me? Because if you think I could do such a thing, then I don't want to see you anymore, and I'll walk home right now." She took the flask out of her bag, then unscrewed the cap.

The pine-needle smell of the liquor filled his head. Shivering, he realized how badly he needed another drink to settle his nerves. "I'm sorry," he said. "Of course I know you wouldn't hurt anybody. It's just that it seemed so *real*."

"I understand. I forgive you." She gave him the flask, and he gulped a long drink. The terror shuddered out of his muscles.

"I guess you were dreaming about the real accident," Joy continued, "but your mind twisted things around."

Real accident? He turned and looked at the Mustang. One headlight was shattered, the fender, crumpled. "Oh, no!" he said.

"It's not as bad as it looks," Joy said. "You can still drive it fine. Which is what you ought to do now. Somebody might have heard the crash, and called the cops."

Peering about, he realized they were trespassing in Riverside Cemetery. Why had they come there? For a moment, the holes in his memory dismayed him, but Joy was right, there was no time to think about it now. They needed to get out of here.

They scrambled back into the car. He put it in gear and twisted the steering wheel, listening for the sound of a tire rubbing, or something banging. To his relief, he didn't hear anything unusual. Joy was right, the vehicle performed as well as ever.

Still, the damage grieved him. He loved the car. And woolly-headed as his mother was, when she noticed the damage, she still might throw a fit. As they passed through the wrought-iron gate, he thumped the steering wheel with the heel of his hand. "Darn it!"

"Take it easy," Joy said. "Have a drink."

He gulped more gin. The liquor took the edge off

his anger, but he was still upset. "I can't believe this happened. I don't have any money to get it fixed."

"You can win it," Joy said. "Remember what I told you about the guys who race for money?"

It took him a moment to figure out what she meant. He wondered why his thoughts were so sluggish. "Old Wilson Highway?"

"Sure," she said. "You still want to, don't you? I thought that's why we went to the graveyard, so you could practice fast starts and turns off the street."

Was that why they'd gone to the cemetery? For a moment, he was sure it wasn't. Then he took another drink, and the booze washed his doubts away.

"I don't know," he said. "If I had a wreck, do I drive well enough to race?"

"Don't be silly," she said. "You didn't have the accident, I did, while I was driving. Don't you remember?" She ran a fingertip along his arm.

And suddenly he did remember, or at least he thought he did. She'd hit a tree or something. "Oh, yeah. Sure. You know, I *am* a good driver. I bet I could beat anybody who lives around here. But how can I win money if I don't have any to bet?"

Joy grinned. "Easy. Bet the car."

He gaped at her. "But what if I lose it? It isn't even in my name."

"Drive fast, and that won't be a problem."

After another drink, he realized she was right.

Twenty-two

Karen awoke drifting in cool darkness. At first, the feeling was so pleasant that she only wanted to enjoy it. Then she realized she was sinking in water. Some instinct had made her hold her breath, even when she was semiconscious, but if she didn't reach air soon, she was going to drown.

She swam for the surface, then remembered how she'd landed in the river in the first place. Joy! What if Joy was watching for her head to bob up?

Well, since Karen had to breathe, she'd just have to risk it, hope the ghost girl wasn't looking, and that her erratic sixth sense was switched off again. Her lungs nearly bursting, Karen shot up into the air, trying to splash as little as possible.

Joy *was* standing on the bank, with Mike at her side, but she seemed to be staring at the wrong section of river. She must not realize how swiftly the current could carry someone downstream.

Karen sucked in a deep breath, dove, and breast-stroked farther down river. When she'd used up all her air, she surfaced again.

The dark figures on the riverbank were gone. A motor growled, the sound fading as it moved away.

Karen paddled to the shore. Now that the immediate danger was past, her body felt numb and feeble. Gripping weeds and tree roots, she dragged herself out of the water, then lay shivering and gasping.

After a while, her terror dimmed, and she started thinking sensibly again. She realized she ought to find out how badly the collision had injured her.

To her amazement, it hadn't hurt her much at all. She was only a bit more bruised and scraped than before. Evidently, because she'd been trying to jump out of the way, and Mike had jerked the steering wheel, the car had only struck her a glancing blow.

She realized she'd been lucky twice, once in the library and once tonight, and there was no reason to expect the luck to hold a third time. Maybe she should give up while she was still alive. If she did, wasn't there still at least a chance that Joy would leave her alone?

A wave of anger washed the temptation away. Even dead drunk and hypnotized, Mike had tried to save her. She couldn't quit on him now.

Which meant she'd have to break into the house on Cross Road and find the anchor.

Karen crawled to the top of the riverbank, stood up, and hurried to the wall. Abandoning the shovel, which she no longer expected to need, she heaved her bike over the barrier, scrambled over herself, then rode away.

As she pedaled through the darkness, it occurred to her that it might help if she could figure out what she was looking for.

Well, Jenny had said that if the anchor wasn't Joy's corpse, it was a treasured personal possession, and that Karen probably saw its duplicate when the phantom appeared. Karen pictured the ghost girl in her mind. Joy wasn't wearing any jewelry, no rings, necklace, or hairclip, but she always materialized in that same shiny red dress. And of course she always carried the silver flask she used to get Mike drunk. Surely, the anchor was one of those two items.

But could Karen find it, among all the possessions that the Carrier family had accumulated over the decades? It would be like looking for a needle in a haystack.

When she reached the house, she saw that Edwina Carrier had let the property go to seed. The hedges had grown wild, nearly sealing the ends of the driveway and the walk. The yellow grass was knee-high. Among the treetops loomed a gabled roof with some of its shingles missing. Paint hung from the walls in long strips, reminding her of a snake shedding its skin. Shutters hung askew. A sign in the front yard announced that the government would auction the house and its contents in two weeks.

As she climbed off her bike and stood it beside the hedge, Karen shivered. The house looked like a worse deathtrap than the library or the cemetery. And I *have* to go in there, she thought.

Or did she? Maybe she could burn it down. No, that was too chancy. Suppose the anchor wound up unharmed, but buried under tons of rubble. She'd never find it then.

She crept up the walk to the pillared porch, resisting an impulse to hunch her shoulders. She thought — hoped — that Joy believed her dead and was off riding with Mike, but she kept imagining eyes staring at her anyway.

The door and ground-floor windows were locked. She used the crowbar to smash a windowpane, wincing at the crash. But she didn't think anyone would hear. The trees and hedges would deaden the noise, and the nearest homes weren't that close.

A faint scent of decay wafted out of the broken window. She reached through, breaking cobwebs and disturbing dusty curtains, unlocked the window, lifted it, and clambered inside.

Twenty-three

The Mustang sped down Old Wilson Highway, its single headlight probing the darkness. Peering dubiously ahead, Mike said, "I don't think there's anybody out here, just fields and barns."

Joy sighed. "Maybe not. But let's go a little farther." Her cool fingers squeezed his. The car started around a curve. Then — "Look!"

Startled, he stomped on the brake. The Mustang fishtailed and swerved left of center. Fortunately, there was no traffic coming the other way. As he veered back into the proper lane, he saw what had excited her: a ramshackle tavern.

"Stop here?" he asked.

"Yes," she said. He turned into the gravel parking lot. "This is where the racers meet — where they used to meet — well, not this building, but another roadhouse on the same spot."

There were only a few other cars in the lot. Mike stopped the Mustang beside one of them, then turned to look at his companion. "What are you talking about?" he asked. She seemed to know so much about this place, it was almost creepy.

The pale girl blinked. "I was just repeating what I heard."

"You must have heard a lot, to be so sure, at first glance in the dark —"

"So maybe I'm not sure," Joy said. "But it'll be easy

to find out." She handed him the flask. "Have another snort, then we'll go inside."

He gratefully raised the bottle to his lips. By the time he lowered it, he'd forgotten that she'd spooked him.

As he climbed out, he stumbled. But somehow Joy had already circled the Mustang, and she caught his arm and steadied him. Hand in hand, they walked toward the bar, gravel crunching under their feet.

The tavern turned out to be grubby and uninviting. The stuffy air smelled of cigarette smoke and stale beer. Burns and patches mottled the coin-operated pool table, and half the lights on the jukebox had gone out. For a moment, Mike wished he'd gone to the Nightmare Club, where things were nice, and he might have found some of his friends. But of course, that was stupid. He hadn't come here for the atmosphere, and Joy was the only *real* friend he had.

The bartender, a barrel-chested man in black-rimmed glasses and a stained white apron, turned toward the door. Abruptly reminded that he was underage, Mike held his breath until he was sure the guy wasn't going to order him out or demand to see ID.

Joy nudged Mike forward. "Go," she whispered. "Talk to him."

"You know more about this than I do," he replied. "Why don't you do it?"

She grimaced. "Because you're the man. You're the one racing. Don't be chicken."

"All right," he said. She sat down at a table by the wall and he walked to the bar. "Two gins, please."

"A double?" the bartender asked.

"No," Mike said, wondering if the man was deaf. "Two gins."

The bartender shrugged. "Whatever." He poured the drinks. The scent of the liquor filled Mike's head. His mouth ached with anticipation. "Three dollars."

Mike dug the last of his cash out of his wallet, then gulped a mouthful of booze. "Look," he said, lowering his voice, "do people race around here?"

The bartender eyed him. "From time to time. What's it to you?"

"I want to do it."

The barman said, "Look, kid, I sold you drinks even though you look polluted, because what do I care? But let me give you some advice. You don't need to race, at least not tonight."

The bartender was trying to tell him what to do. Annoyed, he opened his mouth to tell him to mind his own business. A hand fell on his shoulder.

Startled, he jerked around. One of the other customers had slipped up behind him. The newcomer was a skinny guy two or three years older than him. His nails were black with grease, and tattoos of skulls and daggers crawled up his forearms. His breath smelled of anchovies. Grinning, he said, "I can get you a race."

The bartender said, "Come on, Donnie, give him a break. You can see—"

"Like you said, you're not his mother," Donnie answered. "So butt out."

"Do you want to race me?" Mike asked.

Donnie shook his head. "Not me. My car's a piece of crap. But my buddy Vince will."

"Last I heard, Vince didn't race for fun," the bartender said. "And this guy doesn't have any more money, do you, kid?"

"I'll bet my car," Mike said. As soon as the words were out of his mouth, he wanted to take them back. He told himself not to be a wuss. "It's a '68 Mustang. The body needs work, but it runs good. It's worth a thousand dollars easy."

Donnie said, "Things are a little tight this week. We can only go seven hundred."

From her seat, Joy nodded vigorously. Mike said, "I

139

guess that will be all right."

Donnie slapped him on the back. "Cool! Bob, give my friend here whatever he wants. Put it on my tab. I'm going to call Vince." He strode to the pay phone.

Mike carried the gins to the table. "Well, it's set."

"I heard," Joy said. "I am so proud of you. This Vince clown will never know what hit —" She grunted and clutched her temples.

"What is it?" Mike asked. "What's wrong?"

When she lifted her head, her face was contorted with rage. He blanched, momentarily sure that he'd been dating some sort of maniac. "She's alive," Joy whispered. "She's in my house."

"What? Who's alive?"

The pale girl started to snarl an answer, then faltered. She labored to smooth her face into a smile. "I'm sorry," she said. "For a moment, I didn't feel well. I didn't know what I was saying."

"If you're sick, I'll take you home." He realized that a part of him, the wuss part, he supposed, was eager for an excuse to back out of the race.

"No!" she said. "I do have to go, but alone. I'll be back as soon as I can."

"You're still talking crazy," he said. "We're out in the country. Wherever you want to go, it's too far to walk."

She gripped his hand. He gasped. Her fingers were icy cold. Her black eyes bored into his. "Listen to me. You have to race *now,* so you can fix the car before your mother notices the damage. So stay here, and don't worry about me."

He felt as if all the thoughts in his head were swirling together. "All right," he mumbled.

"Good boy." Her cold lips kissed him, his eyes closed, and then she was gone.

Twenty-four

Karen edged to the door, then groped at the section of wall beside it. After a moment, she found a light switch, and flipped it. The house stayed dark. The electricity must be off.

Fortunately, the full moon shone through the grimy windows, and of course, she had her flashlight. She clicked it on.

The beam revealed a living room crammed with faded antique furniture. Yellowed doilies lay on the arms of the chairs, and embroidered pillows sat on the couch. Bric-a-brac—porcelain figurines, unwound clocks, silver-framed photos, and vases full of artificial flowers—covered every shelf and tabletop. Peering through the doorways to other rooms, Karen could see that the rest of the house was similarly cluttered.

It could take forever to find the anchor if she just sifted through all this junk at random. She needed a plan of attack. She closed her eyes and tried to think.

Joy had died seventy years ago. There was a good chance that her stuff wasn't sitting out anymore. The family had probably packed it up for storage. If so, where would they stick it? If they were like most people, the basement or the attic. So Karen would search those places first. She'd have to find the stairs.

141

As she turned, flashlight in one hand, crowbar in the other, she noticed a photo on the mantel. Joy, with a girl two or three years younger, a chubby man in wire-rimmed glasses, and a gentle-looking woman in pearls. Undoubtedly, her sister and parents. All four were beaming as if they didn't have a care in the world.

To Karen's surprise, she felt a pang of sympathy for Joy, killed so senselessly, so young. She did her best to quash it. It was a bad idea to feel sorry for such a dangerous enemy. It might undermine her determination.

She made a circuit of the ground floor. Discovered stairs leading up, but none that went down. Good, there wasn't any basement. If her reasoning was correct, that narrowed the location of the anchor down to somewhere in the attic.

She set her foot on the first riser. A beam creaked overhead. She froze.

After a second, when the sound didn't repeat, she told herself, that wasn't Joy. It's just the house settling. Then the ceiling groaned again. This time, the rhythm of footsteps was unmistakable.

Karen almost bolted. But she couldn't run now that she was close to the anchor. Joy might kill Mike or her before she made it here again. She had to press on, and hope to stay hidden from the ghost girl.

And she couldn't play hide and seek with a light burning in her hand. She switched the flashlight off.

The stairs were in the center of the house, away from any windows. Without the light, she was blind. When the darkness pressed in on her, she felt even more vulnerable than she had before. She wondered if Joy could see in the dark. Or if, this time, she'd be able to zero in on her with her mind.

Maybe not, or the ghost girl would have come

right to her. Perhaps Joy had gone to the anchor first, to make sure it was undisturbed, and now she was seeking Karen from the top of the house to the bottom.

Karen decided to hide till she heard Joy come down the stairs, then sneak up them. She stowed the flashlight in one of the zippered pockets of her jacket, then tiptoed away, wincing every time a floor-board squeaked, or her leg bumped a piece of furniture. Her groping hand found a cabinet, and she hunkered down behind it.

"Karen." Joy's voice seemed to come from everywhere. The live girl started violently, bit back a whimper. "Come out, come out, wherever you are."

Come get me, Karen thought grimly. Floating dust almost made her sneeze.

"Don't be stupid," Joy continued. "I had to run miles to get here. That was tiring, even for me, so I'm mad. Don't make me madder, or I'll kill you slowly and painfully. Heck, you might as well give up, because Mike is already as good as dead anyway. He's about to drag race drunk, crash, and die. Even if you put an end to me right now, which you won't, it wouldn't save him."

I don't believe you, Karen thought. And even if it's true, Mike might not wreck. There's still a chance. She peeked around the cabinet, squinting, straining to see *something*. Abruptly, gray blobs floated in the blackness. She froze, terrified that she was seeing Joy's white face and hands, then realized that her eyes were playing tricks on her.

The stairs groaned. A moment later, Karen heard Joy step onto the floor. "Last chance to make it easy on yourself," the phantom said, her voice still coming from everywhere at once. "All right, we'll do it your way." Her footsteps creaked toward the front of the house.

Karen counted to ten, then rose, felt her way around the cabinet, and skulked forward, terrified every second that she was about to trip over something. She swept her outstretched hand back and forth, seeking the staircase's banister. Why couldn't she find it? Had she gotten turned around? No, that was dumb, she—

Cold fingers closed about her wrist and yanked her into an embrace. "You shouldn't believe everything you hear," Joy said. Tiny, squirming objects pattered down from her body onto the floor.

Karen shrieked and jabbed with the crowbar. The blow broke Joy's hold. Thrown off balance by the sudden release, Karen stumbled backward and fell, losing her grip on the tool. The crowbar clanged to the floor. The ghost giggled, then the live girl heard her run at her.

Karen tried to roll aside, but she was too slow. Evidently little hampered by the dark, the spirit dove on top of her. Icy hands closed around her throat.

Karen punched and scratched, to no avail. Pressure mounted inside her chest. Then she felt the hilt of the survival knife digging into her side.

The weapon was trapped beneath her. She bucked, jerked it free. Karen unsnapped the strap that held it in its sheath, yanked it out, and slashed.

The blade dragged across Joy's arm. She hissed, and her iron grip loosened. Karen grasped the knife in both hands and stabbed.

The point punched into something solid. The fingers grasping Karen's neck let go, and the mass pressing her down dissolved. Cold liquid ran down the knife and over her hands, then evaporated.

Shaking and gasping, she sat up. She listened and heard nothing.

She supposed it made a weird kind of sense that she could cut Joy. After all, she'd struck the ghost

144

before. And it was logical that the pale girl would have to *become* solid to move solid objects.

But if a person could kill a spirit with a weapon, then why did Karen have to find the anchor?

In the next room, someone moaned.

And abruptly, Karen understood. When Joy was solid, she could be hurt. Stopped for a little while. But no matter how many times someone killed her, she'd always come back.

Still, maybe Karen could get to the attic before the ghost could close in on her again. She leaped up and ran, praying that she hadn't lost her bearings, that the stairs really were in front of her.

Something tripped her. She crashed down, then kicked madly. Finally she realized that Joy hadn't grabbed her ankle. She'd caught her foot on the edge of the bottom step.

She scrambled upward, tripping twice more but never quite falling again. There was pale gray light on the second-floor landing from the moon shining through the bedroom windows and doorways. It was the most beautiful sight she'd ever seen.

Not that there was time to savor it. Joy could be right behind her. She whirled.

The stairs were empty.

And they didn't continue upward. Panting, Karen peered about, frantically searching for the way into the attic. Finally, she saw a panel in the hallway ceiling. It had a handle set in one end, and probably turned into steps when someone pulled it down. She scurried toward it.

A mirror on the wall glowed. Startled, Karen froze, and images formed in the glass. Sweaty and slack-faced, Mike slumped behind the wheel of the Mustang. The picture shifted, revealing that the old Ford sat beside a white Trans Am on a two-lane country road. A skinny guy with tattooed arms raised a handkerchief over his head, then swung it down. The cars shot forward.

The Trans Am took the lead at once. Behind it, the Mustang whipped from side to side, evidently trying to pass. The white car zigzagged with it, holding it back. Finally Mike swerved off the pavement.

Apparently he hadn't seen how close the ditch was to the road. Suddenly the Mustang was flipping through the air. It smashed down on its roof, then started burning.

Karen's view shifted again. Now she was peering through the Mustang's shattered windshield. Mike sprawled upside down, broken bones sticking through his skin, his face a mask of blood. His shirt caught fire.

"This is a live broadcast," Joy said, her voice whispering from the corners of the hall. "Mike's really dying, right now."

"No!" Karen cried. "It's just an illusion!" She slammed the butt of her knife against the mirror, shattering it. Mike's death played on, tiny but distinct, in the bits of glass remaining in the frame. Joy laughed, a screech so loud it hurt the live girl's ears.

Then, suddenly, Joy was on the landing. Her face was crimson bone, and maggots wriggled in her hair. With her red-nailed hands raised, she pounced.

Karen slashed. The knife clipped off two of Joy's fingertips. The ghost girl wailed and stumbled.

Karen sprang, stabbing wildly. She slammed into Joy. The knife grated on bone, then she and the ghost tumbled to the floor. Rearing up, Karen looked down—

And saw a girl with a white, heart-shaped face and a tiny scar on her forehead goggling up at her in terror. "Don't hurt me!" the pale girl babbled. "Please, don't hurt me!"

Not good enough, Karen thought. Even when

146

you're fleshy-faced, I know you're still a ghost. She ripped the knife across Joy's throat. Cold blood spurted. The phantom thrashed, then disappeared.

Karen wanted to lie on the floor and cry. But she raised herself anyway because she knew the fight wasn't over. It would never be over until she destroyed the anchor.

She dragged down the attic steps and scrambled up them. The attic was dark. There were only two windows, each just a few inches across. Karen fumbled the flashlight out of her jacket, turned it on, and then saw how many boxes and trunks were stored there.

Below her, Joy moaned.

Many of the boxes were unmarked. There was no time to open them; Karen just had to hope that Joy's stuff *was* labeled. And finally, the flashlight beam fell on a black steamer trunk decorated with the tarnished brass initials *J. A. C.* Karen tried to lift the lid. It was locked.

She'd lost the crowbar, but she thought the heavy survival knife might work. She jammed it under the lid and pried with all her might.

She heard Joy stumble to her feet.

The trunk flew open. Frantically, Karen rooted through the contents. Antique dolls. A hairbrush and comb. A cut-glass atomizer. A teddy bear. Bracelets. Musty-smelling clothes. No red dress, but finally, at the very bottom, the dull gleam of tarnished silver.

The attic steps creaked.

Crouching low, praying that Joy wouldn't spot her in time to stop her, Karen set the flask on the floor. She tore open another jacket pocket, yanked the lighter fluid out, popped the cap off, and tried to douse the anchor. Her hands were shaking so badly that the first squirt missed, spattering a cardboard box instead.

Floorboards squeaked; the sounds were coming closer.

When the flask was finally soaked, Karen found her matches, tore one out of the book, and struck it. It wouldn't light. She threw it away and ripped out another. It wouldn't ignite either.

Come on, she thought, *please!* I know I was in the river, but this coat is supposed to be waterproof.

As if someone heard her silent plea, the third match burst into flame. She bent to touch it to the flask.

A blow slammed into the side of her head, tumbling her to the floor. The match flew out of her hand. Instead of touching the flask, it hit the fluid-soaked carton, igniting it instantly.

Karen tried to snatch the knife up, but she was too slow. Joy dove on top of her, gripped her throat, and began to strangle her. Fire leaped from one old, dry box to the next, hissing and crackling along the floor.

Twenty-five

Mike swayed in his seat, humming along with the Beatles oldie playing on the jukebox. Whenever he opened his eyes and spied another drinker, he grinned at him, because he could tell the other customers here were nice, just like the bar itself was a friendly place. He'd never felt more at home.

A male voice said, "You ready to roll?"

Mike turned. Two guys stood looking down at him. One was thin, with tattooed arms. For a moment the teenager didn't recognize him, then remembered he was Donnie. And the blond, body-builder type in the blue muscle shirt must be Vince, the guy he'd offered to . . . race?

For a moment, he felt confused, scared, then a wave of confidence washed his anxiety away. Of course, race. He was going to cream this guy. Joy said so. "You got it," he said. "I'm ready to rock and roll." He scooted his chair back from the table. Somehow, it tumbled over, dumping him on the floor. It was really pretty funny. Chuckling, he climbed unsteadily to his feet.

Vince frowned at Donnie. "Jeez, man."

Donnie shrugged. "I didn't tell him how much to drink. Anyway, you want to win, don't you?"

"I guess," the weight-lifter said. He looked at Mike. "If you're sure you're up for it."

Mike scowled. Here was somebody else hinting that he couldn't take care of himself. "I told you, yes. You better worry about yourself. You better be sure you've got my seven hundred ready to hand over."

Vince shrugged his massive shoulders. "Whatever you say. We usually race from here to the Cooper Dairy billboard. The one with the cow wearing the crown. Is that okay?"

"Sure," Mike said.

"Donnie can start us, or we can find somebody else. Whatever you want."

"Donnie's okay."

"Then let's do it." Vince and Donnie turned and walked to the door. Mike hastily grabbed his glass, gulped the last of his drink, and followed them out.

As he wove his way to the Mustang, he looked for Joy, but there was no sign of her. Too bad. She was the one who'd convinced him that he drove well enough to race, so she ought to be here to share the excitement. Oh, well. Next time.

He had trouble putting the key into the ignition. Once again, he felt a pang of disquiet, but another swell of exuberance drowned it. Eventually he got the car started, then pulled out onto the highway beside Vince.

The body-builder was driving a white Trans Am. He revved his engine. Mike did the same. Donnie, standing on the side of the road, lifted a handkerchief, then swept it down like a flag.

The two cars hurtled forward. Working the gearshift frantically, Mike accelerated faster than he ever had in his life. The Trans Am surged ahead of him anyway.

Mike swerved left to pass. The white car veered, too, blocking his path.

Over the next several seconds, he tried repeatedly to pass. Vince cut him off every time. And gradually, the teenager's confidence crumbled into fear. He'd bet his *car,* a car that really belonged to his mom, and he was losing.

No. He *refused* to lose. If he couldn't pass on the road, he'd go off it. Vince wouldn't be expecting that. With his headlight gone and sweat stinging in his eyes, he couldn't really see what lay beside the pavement. But there must be a strip of grass. He down-shifted and jerked the wheel.

Twenty-six

Karen's sight dimmed. She thrashed, scratched, and punched, but couldn't break Joy's stranglehold. She sensed that in another second or two, the terrible pressure would crush her windpipe.

She peered desperately about, finally spotting the lighter fluid-soaked flask, golden now with reflected fireglow, lying near her foot. She writhed and kicked it toward one of the burning boxes.

The bottle stopped a few inches short.

Joy must have heard it scrape along the floorboards. She glanced over her shoulder, cried out, released Karen, and scrambled toward it.

Karen gasped in a breath. The smoky air seared her lungs. As she lurched up, coughing, heat scorching her skin, she saw that most of the attic was already in flames.

She had to get out of there! Still coughing, she started for the stairs, then glimpsed movement from the corner of her eye.

She whirled. Joy was scooping up the flask and running toward the nearby window. No doubt the ghost girl intended to smash the glass and throw the anchor clear of the blaze.

Karen ran at her and tackled her. They landed beside a patch of flame. Karen punched Joy's bloody skull-face, then snatched the flask out of her hand.

The dead girl grappled Karen, slammed her on her back. Now Karen's head was almost *in* the blaze. She felt her hair singeing. In another instant, it would burst into flame.

She forced herself to ignore that and focus on Joy instead. The ghost girl was grabbing for the flask. Karen knocked her hand away, then lobbed the bottle into the fire.

Joy screamed. Her head and shoulders burst into flame. Karen hurled the burning thing off her, scrambled up, and beat frantically at her hair, extinguishing whatever fires were there.

Her entire body ablaze, Joy crawled forward and reached into the fire for the flask. Karen grabbed a broken straight-backed chair, one of the few items that wasn't already burning, and slammed it down on the ghost girl's back.

Joy shrieked. In a sudden flash of heat and glare, her body burned to nothing.

Karen dropped the chair, turned, and stumbled forward. She hoped she was moving toward the stairs; the smoke was so thick and the firelight so dazzling that she couldn't be sure. Starved for air, on the verge of passing out, she scuttled through the maze of burning boxes, looking for a path clear of flame. Once, she lost her balance and nearly plunged headfirst into a stack of burning cartons.

It can't end like this! she thought desperately. I *won!* I'm not going to die in a stupid fire!

She circled one blaze, then another. At last the steps dropped away in front of her. She blundered down them.

The second-floor hall wasn't on fire yet. The air seemed only a little hot and smoky. Karen wanted to drop to her knees and rest, but she knew she didn't dare. Judging from the speed with which the blaze in the attic had spread, the whole house was going to burn, perhaps in a matter of minutes. She had to get out now.

Staggering on, she was horrified to discover that she still felt faint. It was as if the smoke in the attic had poisoned her, and no matter how she gasped at the cleaner air, she couldn't shake off the effects.

She started down the stairs to the ground floor. Her knees went rubbery. Clinging to the banister, she blundered on.

Until suddenly, when she had almost reached the bottom, she realized she wasn't gripping the railing anymore. In fact, she was toppling forward. Her forehead cracked against the floor and a wave of darkness swallowed her.

Twenty-seven

A split second after Mike jerked the steering wheel, he realized that there didn't *have* to be a strip of clear ground beyond the edge of the road. For all he knew, he was hurtling right at a tree. Frantically, he yanked the wheel the other way.

He yanked too hard. The car swerved toward the other side of the highway, and now he could see he was speeding toward a ditch.

He tried to twist the wheel again. His numb hands slipped off it. He grabbed, finally managed to grip it, wrenched. At the same time, his foot fumbled onto the brake.

The Mustang straightened out and lurched to a halt in the center of the road, tires squealing.

Mike switched off the engine, sat in the bucket seat shaking. Suddenly, he could feel how drunk he was, so dizzy that, if he closed his eyes, the world turned somersaults. How could he have ever agreed to race in this condition?

Because Joy had made him. As soon as he thought of her, memories that she'd forced him to forget or ignore began to pop into his head. The near collision on the train tracks. Taking money from his mom's purse. Stealing, running, breaking the bottle over Cope's head in the liquor store. Mindlessly drinking and driving the nights away, constantly risking an accident. Sleeping through the days and missing school. His pale companion appearing and vanishing like a phantom.

The tide of remembered shame and terror churned his stomach. He flung open the door, scrambled out, ran a few steps, and dropped to his knees. The liquor he'd drunk boiled up his throat.

His stomach muscles cramped, and the foul taste seared his mouth, but after he finished puking, his head was clearer. As he raised his head, wiping his lips on his sleeve, he suddenly realized that his peculiar new girlfriend really *had* been a demon, or something else unnatural—something that had been out to destroy him.

For some reason, she must be gone now. Otherwise, he wouldn't be able to think straight. Thank God he was still alive. Thank God he hadn't messed up his life so badly he couldn't straighten it out. He could go back to school, make up with his friends, with Karen—

The jolt of the Mustang hitting Karen, the sight of her body flying into the river, came back to him with hideous clarity. His friend was dead!

No. He didn't know that for sure. He had to get back to the Hollow and find out.

Ahead, the Trans Am braked, U-turned, and sped back down the road. It stopped in front of the Mustang, then Vince climbed out. "What's the problem?" he demanded.

Mike stood up. "I quit, so I guess you win. But I can't pay up. The Mustang isn't mine. I'm sorry." He wondered if the body-builder was going to beat him up. He deserved it.

The big man sighed. "Forget it. I shouldn't have raced you in the first place. Donnie gets too eager to make a score sometimes."

"Thanks." Mike hesitated. "If you're not going to

kill me, could you take me home? I have to get back to the Hollow fast, and I shouldn't drive myself."

Vince laughed. "Jeez, you've got a lot of nerve. Okay, why not?"

Twenty-eight

As Vince turned onto Cross Road, he said, "Something's burning up this way. Should we detour?"

Mike lifted his eyes to peer out the windshield. Ahead and to the left, above the trees and houses, gray smoke and orange sparks rose into the sky.

"Go straight for now," he replied. "If this road's closed, there are plenty of side streets to turn onto."

After another minute, the blaze came into view. Vince slowed down to look at it. A big, two-story house was burning. Flames had all but devoured the second floor, and begun to lick at the first.

The street wasn't blocked; the fire department hadn't arrived yet. Ordinarily, Mike would have been concerned, but the sign in the yard made it clear that the structure was abandoned. So nobody could be in danger.

He said, "When we come to a pay phone, we should call this in. Just in case nobody else has." A shadow beside the house's hedge caught his eye. "Stop the car!"

Vince hit the brakes. "What is it?"

Mike didn't know, except that something about the shape of the shadow alarmed him. He jumped out and dashed toward it.

The heat of the burning house scorched him, even at a distance. The fire roared. The shadow turned out to be a girl's green Schwinn. There were red and white streamers attached to the ends of the handlebars and a curved horn with a black rubber bulb bolted in the middle. Mike had bought that horn himself, in seventh grade, to give as a birthday present.

This was *Karen's* bike. What was it doing here? What if Joy had lured his friend to the house, trapped her inside, then set it ablaze?

"Karen!" he shouted. No one answered.

He ran toward the porch. Flame crawled from the burning roof onto the pillars.

A window beside the door was open. He leapt through and immediately began choking on the smoke on the other side.

Coughing, he blundered through the murk. He was afraid he'd stumble right past his friend without seeing her. Then yellow light flared through a doorway. Mike turned and saw Karen sprawled motionless at the bottom of a staircase. Flame crackled down the risers like a reaching hand.

Mike plunged forward. Straining, weak from the heat and lack of oxygen, he picked Karen up and staggered back to the front of the house.

He fumbled open the door and carried her through. Overhead, something creaked. Somehow he found the strength to leap onto the grass. Behind him, the porch roof collapsed in a rain of blazing rubble.

Vince ran up, took Karen, and draped her over his shoulder. "Come on!" he said, trotting back toward the street. Mike reeled after him.

The body-builder laid Karen on the grass beside the curb. "How'd you know she was in there?" he asked.

159

Mike gasped, "Tell you later. Is she okay?"

Without awakening, Karen coughed. Vince said, "Well, she's breathing, and she isn't burned, so I think so."

Mike said, "Thank God. I was so scared in there. I'm still shaking. I wish I had a drink to calm me down."

"And I guess you've earned one," Vince said. "There's a six-pack in my backseat. Help yourself. I'll watch her."

Gratefully, Mike stumbled to the Trans Am, reached in, and grabbed a can of Budweiser. He popped the top and raised it to his mouth.

And then he realized, here he was, still drunk, a condition that had nearly killed him, but eager to guzzle more. He was jittery, so he'd automatically turned to alcohol to make himself feel better.

Joy hadn't created his drinking problem. She'd preyed on a weakness he'd already possessed but never acknowledged. If he faced it now, got some help for it, he could live the life he wanted to live, maybe even help his mom get her life back together. If he kept denying it, it was going to destroy him as surely as his ghostly companion would have.

He shuddered. Turning the can over, he poured the beer out, just as a high-pitched siren began howling in the distance.

Karen coughed again, then sat up. He ran to her side. "Are you all right?" he cried.

"Yeah," she wheezed. "Are you?"

"Now I am," he said, relief evident on his face.

Looking up, he saw a fire truck rocketing down the road toward them.

Epilogue

A late afternoon breeze blew off the river. It moaned among the tombstones, rattled branches, and made Mike shiver. He released Karen's hand to close the snaps on his Cooper High jacket. She stooped and laid her bouquet of white roses at the foot of the Calvary cross.

Mike said, "You must be the nicest person in the world. After what Joy did to us, I could never forgive her, let alone bring her flowers."

Karen shrugged. "I feel sorry for her. Nobody should die the way she did. I hope I sent her on to someplace where she can heal." She brushed a windblown strand of red hair out of her eyes. "Since you *don't* forgive her, I appreciate you coming with me."

He took her hand. "That's okay. I like being with you, wherever you're going. And it's kind of reassuring to see that Joy's still buried."

Karen snorted. "That makes no sense at all. She was *always* buried."

Mike grinned. "I never said I was logical."

But he *was* happy. In the month since Karen had saved him, he'd managed to stay away from alcohol. As a result, he was looking good on the basketball court. What was more, to his own amazement, he'd finally managed to motivate his mother to do something with her life. She'd just found a part-time job. And of course, his romance with Karen was going great. He didn't have a worry in the world.

Until she murmured, "I wonder if there are any more."

"Any more what?" Mike asked carefully.

"Spirits," she said. "If we could meet one, why not another? After all, the Hollow has a thousand ghost legends—"

"Which are probably all a load of bull," he said. The chill wind whispered. He trembled. "Come on, let's get out of here before it gets any colder."

"Or darker," she replied.

About the Author

RICHARD LEE BYERS is a talented and acclaimed author who holds a B.A. and an M.A. in Psychology. Before becoming a writer, he worked as a psychotherapist and administrator in the mental health field.

When Richard was growing up in Columbus, Ohio, he enjoyed reading classic novels in the genre of the fantastic including H.G. Wells' books *The Time Machine, The War of the Worlds,* and *The Invisible Man,* and Edgar Rice Burroughs' *Tarzan* and *Mars* books. Those works greatly influenced Richard as a writer, as well as books by authors Fritz Leiber, Robert E. Howard, and H.P. Lovecraft.

Richard now resides in the Tampa Bay, Florida area. His recent adult novels include *The Vampire's Apprentice* and *Dead Time.* His short stories have appeared in *Freak Show, Grails: Quests, Visitations, and Other Occurrences, Confederacy of the Dead,* the *Tampa Tribune, 2AM, New Blood, Eldritch Tales, Amazing Experiences,* and *Quick Chills: The Year's Best Horror from the Small Press, Volume One.*

Richard likes to hear from readers. He, and everyone at *The Nightmare Club,* would enjoy hearing how you like the books, and what you'd like to see in future stories. Write to him, c/o The Nightmare Club, Zebra Books, 475 Park Avenue South, New York, NY, 10016. If you'd like a reply, please include a stamped, self-addressed envelope.

SNEAK PREVIEW!
Here is a special preview of the next
Nightmare Club.
The Initiation by Nick Baron is now available!

THE NIGHTMARE CLUB #2
THE INITIATION
Nick Baron

She was seventeen and beautiful. The midnight wind blew her hair into her face. The moonlight caused her skin to glow pale white, her dark eyes to reveal a passionate yearning.

He loved her. As they embraced in the clearing, surrounded by powerful trees whose gently swaying branches seemed to lean in to hear his words, he whispered that he would love her his entire life.

A rustling came from somewhere close. He started, looking around sharply, and drew her into his arms.

"Don't be afraid," she whispered.

"I heard something."

"It's all right. I told you I had a surprise for you."

He looked into her lovely face and was instantly set at ease by her warm and slightly mischievous smile. "I thought maybe you were followed," he said. "I thought it could have been one of the Chalmers' Patrol."

"No," she said. "Don't worry. I've been careful."

She was a junior at the Cooper Riding Academy for Girls. Elise Chalmers ran the school. Curfew was strictly enforced by her staff. Nevertheless, the beautiful young woman he had fallen in love with had managed to sneak away on a regular basis to see him. For this, he felt like the luckiest boy in Cooper Hollow.

"It's time," she said softly. "Do you want your surprise?"

Pulling her close, he kissed her once more. "Yeah, I want my surprise." He shook her playfully, his powerful arms wrapped around her slender waist. "Gimme, gimme, gimme!"

She laughed, "I brought something for you from Cooper.

"Show me."

She held his hand tightly and guided him deep into the woods along a narrow path he had never before noticed. Suddenly, they came upon a magnificent gray horse tethered to a sturdy pine tree. He gasped, his mind unwilling to comprehend the incredible sight.

When he was a child, his family had owned a farm in Virginia. Much of his early childhood had been spent on horseback. When he was nine, the banks drove his parents out. His family moved to Cooper Hollow so that his father could go to work in his brother's insurance firm in the city. Adjusting to life away from the farm had been difficult. For years, he had felt crippled by the loss of his daily rides. When he imagined once again climbing on the back of a sturdy mount, he nursed a phantom pain, as if from a limb that had been painfully severed.

He wanted desperately to tell her that he had never seen a horse so powerful, so majestic, but he knew that if he tried to speak, he would cry. Instead, he squeezed his girlfriend's hand, parted from her, and took a few cautious steps in the animal's direction. Its massive head swiveled around and he was caught by its warm and inviting gaze.

"Come on," his girlfriend said with a wide, amazing smile. "Let's go for a ride."

Nodding, he took a few moments to run his hand over the horse's flank, and eventually allowed it to lick his hand. Pressing his face against its mane, he hugged the animal, then came around and mounted it as if only minutes, not years, had passed since he had last been astride a horse. He watched as his girlfriend untethered the horse. When she was finished, he held out his hand and she climbed on behind him, encircling his waist with her lean but very strong arms, the arms of a horsewoman.

"I know another path," she said. "Once you've got the feel—"

"I love you," he said.

"You, too," she whispered.

With her guidance, they found the path. He had already become attuned to the gray horse's rhythms, and felt comfortable with the animal, confident that it would respond to his every command. He wanted to urge the horse to break into a run, but that would be too dangerous. After they cleared the woods outside the school and reached the bank of the lake, perhaps they could afford to be a little more reckless. For now, they would continue to navigate carefully the tight channels between the closely bunched trees. He was grateful for the advice his girlfriend whispered in his ear. The woods were a labyrinth and he would have been lost without her.

Suddenly, the gray horse stopped.

"What's the matter, Beauty?" he asked. With chilling slowness, the creature turned its head in his direction. Its eyes had become crimson. They blazed, slicing through the darkness like the tips of hot pokers poised to run him through. His instincts told him to dismount instantly, but before he could do so, before he could even speak a warning to his girlfriend, the animal bolted forward. All he could do was put his head down and hug the neck of the creature. He prayed that his girlfriend would not give in to panic. She held onto him as they barreled through the woods, lowlying branches reaching for them, threatening to swipe them off the back of the charging mount. The boy restrained a scream as a skeletal branch grazed his arm, ripping a bloody furrow in his jacket.

The trees they passed on either side seemed a blur. The wind whipped the mane of the gray horse into his face and he was almost overcome by hysteria as he felt the soft hairs tickling his face. The itch that resulted was so terrible he would have done anything short of releasing his grip on the animal to scratch it.

He could feel the beat of a thundering heart pounding against his chest and had no idea if it was his heart or that of the horse. The creature's flesh, however, once hot and vital to his touch, was freezing. His fingers began to tingle, as if he were clinging to a block of ice and might suffer frostbite if he didn't loose his hold.

Still, the boy held on.

Suddenly, with a final rustling like the parting of a veil, they burst through one last thicket of trees and were out of the forest. Now they were racing along the shore of a sparkling lake. The boy's efforts to bring the gray horse under control failed miserably, and his relief at escaping the deadly woods was short-lived. The animal was, impossibly, gaining in speed. The wind kicked against the boy's face and he had to turn his head slightly. The itch

168

was still driving him insane. His only source of comfort was the feel of his girlfriend's arms around him. He had to protect her. Nothing else mattered, not even his own life.

Without warning, the horse came to a full stop and reared up with a cry that was unlike any sound the boy had ever heard. It was a shrill, murderous noise, like nothing human or animal had ever made.

The gray horse bucked and tossed the riders into the air. The boy felt his girlfriend's hands come away from him as they were wrenched from the animal's back. A splash sounded somewhere to his left an instant before he himself struck the icy waters. Then he was in the murky depths, struggling to reach the surface.

Suddenly, his head rose above the water of the lake. He was free, he had survived! His feeling of exultation faded quickly. The horse was gone and there was no sign that his girlfriend had reached the surface. She might not have been thrown so far into the lake; she might have struck her head on a stone in a more shallow part of the water.

Without hesitation, he drew a deep breath and dove under the lake's black surface.

It was the last breath he would ever take.

She waited on the shore. The gray horse stood beside her. She had seen her boyfriend's head emerge briefly. He had looked directly at her, but he had not seen her. Nor had he seen the horse beside her, its flank cold, its fetid breath turning immediately to steam, its red eyes glowing in the darkness. She turned from the creature so that it could not see her tears.

Only a few bubbles marked the spot on the lake

where her boyfriend had gone under for the last time. She knew what he had seen and felt. The strange tugging, then the sight that illuminated the darkened waters, the sight that was enough to drive any mortal insane with its varied and hideous aspects.

Suddenly, a blackish-red geyser spouted from the surface of the lake. Blood and bits of bone rained down, then were immediately sucked below, far below, to the maw of the creature she served.

"Goodbye," she whispered. She was about to add, "I love you, too," when a remarkable sensation coursed through her. The change that had been promised had been enacted. It had been shocking in its swiftness. She was glad that she had not spoken those final words to her dead boyfriend. The Sentinel beside her would have interpreted those words as weakness, and rightly so.

She had passed her Initiation. The fear and regret she felt at the sight of her boyfriend's passing had vanished in an instant, replaced with a numbing sense of purpose, and the first, vague stirring of a remarkable power. Promises had been made to her. She now knew that those promises would be kept. The power she had been told about was *real*.

"Come on," she whispered, turning away from the lake. She did not wait to see if the Sentinel would follow her. It moved behind her as silently as a shadow. "We have a lot to do . . ."

Five months later.

Kimberly Kilpatrick unlocked the door to her private room and went inside. She was wearing her full riding habit — tan riding pants, matching riding jacket, a white shirt, and black knee-high boots.

Her brunette hair had been braided and hidden beneath her black riding helmet, which she now removed and tossed on the bed. Kimberly was trim and only five-foot-three inches tall; nevertheless, the manner in which the seventeen year-old held herself was striking. Kimberly seemed impervious to any outside force. Nothing was further from the truth.

Kimberly's room at the Cooper Riding Academy was considerably more austere than her room at home. Kimberly went now to her plain dresser and opened the middle drawer. Two photographs lay within, one of her real parents, who had died when she was very young, the other of her uncle and his wife, her guardians. Until four months ago, when she had enrolled in Cooper's summer riding classes, Kimberly had lived with them. Now their picture was only brought out when she knew they would be visiting.

The photograph of her real parents meant infinitely more to Kimberly. Carefully, she took it out and looked at it. The reassuring smiles of her mom and dad always made her feel better, no matter how horrible her day had been. In her room at her guardians' house, Kimberly kept entire photo albums devoted to her parents. Her uncle hated when she dragged them out. David and Margaret had not wanted the responsibility of raising a child. Kimberly knew they resented her parents for dying and leaving them with such a burden.

When Kimberly had suggested attending Cooper for her senior year, her aunt and uncle had leapt at the opportunity. What a relief that had been. Anything was better than living with her unloving guardians, or so she had thought at the time.

Kimberly had been an honors student at her last school. At Cooper, she was barely making the grade. She carried five subjects and had at least four hours of homework a night, more on weekends. Recently, she had fallen into the habit of staying up half the night to work with a penlight after "lights out" had been called.

Then there were all the rules of conduct she had been forced to learn. At Cooper, a lapse in protocol was treated like a capitol offense, and her rich, snobbish classmates reveled in reminding her of her mistakes. The teachers were pleasant, but severe. Only Jane Hadrick, the assistant headmistress, had been kind enough to take Kimberly aside and help her through the complexities of her new existence.

Kimberly entered the school as a senior, and that had entitled her to many privileges. But resentment was high from the lower grade students. They had been laboring for years, looking forward to the day when they would have the right to walk on the grass instead of the gravel, the day they would be allowed to step onto the senior staircase, the day they would be treated with awe and respect. Kimberly had just walked in and had it all handed to her.

Those who had come up through the ranks and were Kimberly's "equals" were even harder to handle. In their opinion, there was no such thing as a school that equaled Cooper; the school Kimberly had transferred from had been a *public* high school, for heaven's sake, and her uncle was not even registered in *Who's Who,* the *Blue Book,* or the *Social Registry.* The man's law practice had made him wealthy, but there was wealthy and there was *fabulously wealthy.* Kimberly's uncle simply didn't make the grade, and, therefore, neither did Kimberly.

Still, there was one major advantage in Kimberly's becoming a full-time student at Cooper—the

172

opportunity to ride several times a week. The only time Kimberly felt true freedom was during those precious hours when she was astride one of the academy's powerful mounts. In all her life, *nothing* had ever spoiled that experience. Not until today, at any rate.

Sharon Cruise, a girl who hated Kimberly with a true passion, had talked her father into purchasing the one horse with which Kimberly had bonded. And Sharon had reserved the pleasure of passing on this information to Kimberly for herself.

Kimberly had attempted to show no reaction. She was determined not to give Sharon the pleasure of seeing her tears. But now that she was safely back in her room, holding onto the photograph of her mother and father as if it could protect her, Kimberly threw herself on her bed and wept openly. Lightning had been the closest thing Kimberly had to a friend at the academy. Now even he was gone. It was always the same. Everyone she loved went away.

After a while, Kimberly's tears slowed and she began to think. It *could* be worse, she realized. Though she was considered a reject, it was not as bad as having the honor of being *the* reject, the one that was marked for the year long "Rite of Passage." Another girl, Thelma Hopkins, had been given that honor. Each year, one girl was picked to bear the insults of all the others, to serve them, to be humiliated by them, and to lose all hope of ever being accepted as their equal. Kimberly had been told various horrible stories about the ritual during which this title was bestowed.

From what Kimberly had been able to piece together, the girl was taken from her room, with her mouth taped up so that she couldn't scream, and a pillowcase thrown over her head so that she couldn't see where she was being led. When the girls arrived at the destination, the pillowcase was removed from the victim's head so that she could see her surroundings—usually some dark, smelly place, possibly a furnace room, and packed with dozens of her classmates. She would be forced to perform rituals—some said she would be told to act like an animal. Then she would be beaten and her hair would be chopped short to indicate her new station. Then the girl was warned that if she made any attempt to tell Ms. Chalmers or the other teachers about what had happened, she would be severely punished.

To date, not one of the girls who had been marked for the "Rite of Passage" had made it through the entire academic year without being transferred to another school. But that was all part of the plan. Only the girls who were hated the most, those whose presence was no longer desired, were given this treatment.

Kimberly wiped away the last of her tears. She felt guilty at being relieved that someone else would suffer this fate. *No one* should have to go through anything like the "Rite of Passage." Still, with all of her own problems, she could not help but be grateful that she had not been targeted for this "honor."

Kimberly found herself beginning to relax. The past week had been hellish; waiting for Sharon's next prank or punishment had made her tense. Its arrival had almost come as a relief.

No, that wasn't right. She could not allow herself to be relieved at the thought of Lightning in the hands of Sharon's family. Her parents seemed oblivious to their daughter's faults. Sharon had probably whined and pleaded with her daddy to buy her the horse but now that she had him, Kimberly was sure she'd neglect him terribly.

The spoiled little witch, Kimberly thought. Sharon would grow tired of the animal soon enough and her parents would sell him to someone else, certainly at a profit.

Rising, Kimberly left the photograph of her parents on the bed and went back to her small dresser, where her stuffed bear from her childhood sat. It was a silly blue bear with a big white stomach. She touched its smiling face. Her parents had given her this bear. Or, they had meant to, anyway.

Kimberly thought again of the day on which her parents had died. She was a child, a day away from her ninth birthday. She had spent the entire Saturday afternoon in her parents' restaurant, playing as they labored to get the place ready for the dinner rush. She remembered that she had hounded them, begged them to tell her what gifts she would be getting for her birthday.

At one point a ball she had been bouncing off the wall behind the building had fallen down the basement stairs. She chased it underground where she smelled something funny.

Kimberly retrieved the ball and went back upstairs. She remembered she was about to tell her father about the smell, when she spotted a shiny blue bicycle in the middle of the restaurant. Her mom and dad stood beside it, grinning from ear to ear. Tom Kilpatrick said, "We thought we'd give you one present early."

All thoughts of the terrible smell were driven from her head. She laughed and squealed excitedly, and was overjoyed when her mom told her that she could go outside and try it out, if she wanted.

Kimberly had taken the bicycle out of the restaurant and was two blocks away, pedaling as fast as she could, when a muffled bang sounded from the

175

direction of her parents' restaurant. Kimberly stopped the bike. Turning, she saw a black cloud of smoke rise up into the air like an angry fist. Kimberly raced back to the restaurant, but it was too late. The place was on fire. She tried to run inside, but one of the people in the crowd that had sprung from nowhere grabbed her and hauled her back.

Years later, Kimberly learned that what she smelled in the basement was gas. If she had warned her parents, they might have gotten out of the restaurant alive. But she had been thinking only about her wonderful new bicycle. Her parents had paid the price for her greed.

If only I could see you, Kimberly thought, her fingers running over the furry belly of her little blue bear. It was one of the other presents her parents had been planning to give her for her ninth birthday. Tears welled in Kimberly's eyes.

"I wish I could talk to you one more time," she whispered. "Tell you I'm sorry. Say goodbye."

She picked the bear up and hugged it to her. Then, she frowned. Something was horribly wrong with the stuffed animal. It was heavy and it *squished* as she pressed it tightly against her chest. She was dimly aware of a cold, wet substance leaking down her arms, and when she looked down, she saw something that couldn't possibly be real.

With a scream, Kimberly dropped the bear. It struck the floor and exploded with a muffled *plop*. The seam that had been holding it together tore open and a grotesque collection of blood-drenched intestines and internal organs splattered onto the floor. Blood was on the front of her uniform, on her hands, her arms.

Kimberly felt ill and choked back her urge to vomit, aware that she would raise her bloody hands to her mouth to do so which would make it all the worse. Belief in what was before her came slowly. She felt light-headed and dazed.

This can't be happening, she thought. No one could do something like this. It wasn't human.

Suddenly, she heard the door to her room swing open. Apparently, she had not closed it all the way. It would have locked if she had. Someone was in the room. Hands were on her arms. Kimberly was turned away from the sight of her precious little blue bear, her bleeding little blue bear. A regular drip of crimson came from its small bow tie, which read, "best friends."

"Oh God, oh please, no," Kimberly muttered. Her mind was not ready to accept anything like this. How could anyone have been so cruel?

Then she realized that more than one person had entered the room. At least five girls had crowded in. One of them carried a white pillowcase. Kimberly recognized two of the girls as Sharon's friends.

She tried to pull away from them, but it was too late and there were too many of them. Her hands were yanked behind her back with enough force to cause Kimberly real pain. Kimberly saw Sharon leaning casually in the doorway, arms crossed, a wicked smile on her lips.

Sharon laughed. "It just hasn't been your day, has it, Kilpatrick? Look at it this way: Because of you, at least one person is going to have a good year after all."

LOOK FOR THE NIGHTMARE CLUB'S
THE INITIATION,
NOW AVAILABLE!

WANTED TO RENT by Jessica Pierce

Sixteen year-old Christy Baker thinks it's totally
unfair that her mother wants to rent out her bedroom to help make ends meet. But now Christy's
really worried. There's something about their handsome boarder, Ethan Palmer, that gives her the
creeps. Things get even creepier when she finds
some strange items hidden in his bedroom. A
coiled length of rope . . . a roll of masking tape
. . . newspaper clippings about recently murdered
women. *And* . . . a photo of herself!

Now Christy is home alone. The downstairs door
has just opened. She knows who's come in—and
why he's there!

BLOOD PACT by Debra Franklin

When Jamie Fox and her friends learn the abandoned train depot where they hang out is about to
be demolished, they decide to take action. Forming
a "suicide" pact, they sign their names in blood,
vowing to kill themselves to keep the depot intact.
Of course, they never really intended to carry out
the pact . . .

Then, one by one, those who signed the blood
pact, begin to die. The deaths are labeled suicides,

but Jamie suspects her friends are really being murdered. Now she must unmask a cunning killer who's watching *her* every move. If she doesn't, she'll be the next to die!

DEADLY DELIVERY by Michael August

It's just another long, hot summer—until Derek Cliver and his friends join an exciting new mail-order club. The Terror Club allows Derek and his friends to create their own monsters. *And* it gives them the opportunity to "dispose" of those they despise most. But the game turns terrifyingly real when the monsters they create come to life—and actually murder their rivals.

Now, as the body count rises, Derek and his friends must somehow undo what they've done . . . before they become the next victims!

SCREAM!
WANTED TO RENT
Jessica Pierce

Christy Baker couldn't afford a new pair of shoes. That's how tight money had been for them since her parents' divorce. Five months, thought Christy, and nothing seems any better. She worried her finger into a small hole in the sole of her Adidas, then took it out again before she made things worse. It wasn't just the hole she minded. The shoes had begun to squeak when she walked through the halls between classes. Everybody could hear them. It was embarrassing. She'd tried stuffing paper in the foot of them, but that didn't help. It only made her feet sore.

The shoes would have to last a little longer. Christy couldn't ask for money to replace them, no matter how much she hated the old shoes. Not this week. Her mom was having enough troubles with her job right now, dealing with layoffs at the library, without Christy making the situation any worse at home.

Her mom looked so tired most of the time. It hadn't always been like this. When her mom and dad were still married, Christy and Charlotte, her ten year-old sister, saw a lot of their parents. Not together, but at least they saw them. Since the divorce, Christy barely spoke to her dad. He had moved out of state the week after he left home. She talked to him on the phone sometimes, but it wasn't the same.

The hours that her mom was home seemed to be occupied with studying computer files she brought from work. People were losing their jobs, and she was the head librarian. It was up to her to find a way to spread around the available hours and keep the library from losing any more of its staff to the unemployment lines.

That was the real fear—unemployment. It could happen to them, too.

"I don't know if we should try to stay here," Christy's mom confided to Christy one night. She was writing checks for a stack of bills in front of her. "The house payment takes so much of my check each month, and with everything else, I don't know if we can afford it much longer."

Christy had been scraping cat food into Tippy's bowl outside the front door. The cat was purring and rubbing against her legs, wanting attention. It was hard to ignore him, but she kept being drawn back to the way her mother's expression changed when she was paying bills. There were new worry lines around her mom's eyes, and a tired kind of frown that seemed to pull at her mouth like a weight. Her mom was usually a very attractive woman, tall and thin, with a nice face, pretty green eyes, and neatly cut brown hair that curled under just below the nape of her neck. Lately, she just looked worried.

On another night, Christy had watched from the doorway as her mother picked up a bill, held the envelope for several minutes as if thinking what to do with it, and then put the bill down again in the same pile, letting it go unpaid for another month.

With that kind of pressure over money, new shoes could wait.

What Christy didn't want, was to lose the house. That would mean moving away from school and her friends. She didn't think she could handle that. Her friends were all that kept her from losing it these last few months. They had been there for her when her dad left. Some of them knew what that experience was like. Their parents had split up, too.

Whatever else she had to give up, Christy decided, she couldn't lose the house. It was hard enough trying to keep up her grades this year, without thinking about changing schools in mid term. She might be ready to live someplace else when it came time for college, but not in the middle of her junior year.

"Christy." Her mother called from the bottom of the stairs.

"Up here, Mom."

A soft knock sounded on the bedroom door a couple of minutes later. Her mother always knocked, thank God, and didn't read Christy's mail, either. In general, her mom was a lot better than some of the mothers of Christy's friends. Privacy was important. Some parents didn't respect their kid's rights. Christy's mom had always been really good about things like that. Not so good at making a marriage work, but in respecting her daughter's privacy, she got an A.

"Come in," Christy called from the bed. She was stretched full length in a corner-to-corner angle across her bed, school textbook held in one hand, and a bowl of chips in the other.

Her mother opened the door. "How can you concentrate on what you're reading?" her mom asked, reaching to turn down the volume on the stereo. Her mother claimed it was impossible to read and listen to music at the same time.

"It's not a problem."

"At least turn it down a little."

"Okay." It was easier to give in.

Her mom had worry lines at the corners of her eyes again. She sat on the edge of Christy's bed, sighing, and looking as if she didn't know where she should go from here. She was holding a folded newspaper in her hands.

"You okay?"

"Hmm?" asked Mom. "Oh, yes. Sure. It's just . . . I have something I need to talk to you about, that's all."

The last time a conversation started like this, her dad had left them. Only bad news was announced before anybody said it. This "talk" had all the signs of bad news coming fast. She glanced again at the newspaper in her mother's hand, the classifieds, and guessed.

"We're moving?" Christy's heart sank with the words.

"Moving?" Her mom seemed surprised. "No. That's what I've been trying to avoid. I was afraid we might have to sell this place, but . . . what made you think that?"

Christy pointed to the classifieds.

"Oh, right." She tried to pull together a worn-out smile. "Sorry. I guess it did look like that. Here I am trying to break it to you gently," she said, "and I manage to mess everything up, anyway."

Break it to you gently. It wasn't the kind of sentence to fill Christy's heart with confidence.

"What's wrong?" She sounded too blunt, but wanted to know. She was beginning to feel a little sick from trying to guess what her mother was go-

ing to say. "Is it about Dad? He's not hurt or—"
She felt a racing going on in her brain, as if there
were electric currents there, and something had
touched the charges.

"He's fine," her mother said, the words sounding
clipped and resentful. "At least he was, the last time
anyone around here heard from him."

Bringing up Dad had been a mistake.

"Could we turn this off for a minute?" Her
mother's glance took in the stereo.

Christy gave up the battle and switched off the
music.

Mom started talking then, as if she'd been prac-
ticing her lines and knew them by heart. "You
know that I've been trying to think of some way
for us to stay in the house. I wanted you to finish
high school here, with your friends." The words
spilled out in a breathless rush. "There didn't seem
to be any way we could do that, with our financial
situation the way it is at the moment. Then, I
found this."

While Christy watched, her mother unfolded the
newspaper she had clutched in her hand. It was a
page from the classifieds. Circled in ink was an ad
which read:

Wanted to rent. Young seminary student
wishes to rent room in private house,
Walbrook district. Excellent references. Contact: #582, Classifieds

Christy didn't get it at first. What did this ad
have to do with solving their problems? They lived
in Walbrook, but that couldn't be the—

"Christy," her mother blurted out, "I'm renting
him a room. I spoke to him on the phone this
morning, and came home to show him the house at

lunch. He's a very nice man." She went on, "Polite, intelligent, and studying to become a minister. He's earning his degree in theology," she explained, as if Christy might be interested in that. "He liked the room and agreed to move in right away. He gave me an immediate deposit. Christy, it's going to save us. With the money he'll give us for rent, we'll be able to keep the house."

Nothing was making any sense. All she could think to ask was, "What room?"

Her mother acted as if she hadn't noticed the shaking in Christy's voice. "We'll move you in with Charlotte downstairs. There's space enough for two beds, if we push the furniture against the walls. Charlotte will love having the company, and you—"

"Mom!" Christy sat up, spilling chips all over the bed. "You can't rent some stranger *my* room."

Her mother looked at her with innocent eyes. "It's already done," she said. "He's moving in tomorrow."

This couldn't be happening. "I'm sixteen; Charlotte's ten. What about my posters? All the stuff on the walls? My phone? It's my room. I can't move in with Charlotte. I won't."

The look in her mother's eyes told her. She would. There wasn't any choice. Unless they rented the room to this stranger, they couldn't afford to keep the house.

"I'm sorry, Christy. I wish it were different. We have to get started right away, and I need your help. He's going to be here early in the afternoon."

There wasn't anything left to say. Obviously, it didn't matter what Christy thought. She got up and started tearing the posters off the wall. The first one, her favorite, ripped in half when she pulled it. Frustrated and angry, she wadded it up and threw it into the trash.

That was exactly how Christy felt, torn apart and thrown out.

The flowers arrived the next morning, a tall arrangement of pink gladioli, white iris, and delicate sprigs of baby's breath. They were delivered with a card addressed to Laura Baker and children. The card read: "With grateful thanks to my new family."

"I'm not his new family," said Christy. She scratched Tippy behind the ears, and gave him some dry cat food before she closed the front door.

"He's just trying to be friendly," said Mom. "I think it's nice. Such pretty flowers, too." She placed the arrangement on a table in the entry hall. "If we leave them here, he'll see the flowers when he walks in the door. That will make him feel welcome."

"He's not welcome," said Christy, "and I think his flowers are ugly."

Charlotte leaned close and sniffed the blooms. "I can't smell them."

"They're probably phony," said Christy, "like him."

That remark earned her a hard look from her mother. "He's very nice. And I expect you to be nice, too. Understand?"

The doorbell prevented Christy from having to answer.

"Mr. Palmer!" Mom's voice was high and flirty. "Please, come in. Welcome."

When he stepped into the hall, Christy could see why her mother was acting so weird. The man was taller than her dad, about six feet. His hair was light brown, with clean-looking sun streaks shot through it. He was dressed in a pale blue-gray sports coat, gray shirt, and charcoal slacks. His eyes matched the color of the coat, and he had a nice face. The way he looked was a surprise, but the biggest surprise was his age; he had to be in his mid-thirties. Christy had been expecting a student, someone much younger.

"These are my girls," Mom said. "Christy, Charlotte, this is Mr. Ethan Palmer."

"Christy, what a pretty name," he said, stepping closer. He put out his hand.

It would have been rude not to shake hands with him. Christy didn't want to touch him, but when she did, his hand felt warm and strong. "Hi," was all she could manage.

"And you're Charlotte," he turned to her ten year-old sister. "Your mother's told me about both of you, and I see she hasn't polished the truth." He scrunched down a little. "I had a dear friend named Charlotte. You look a little like her. The same blue eyes and sweet face. Even your hair," he said, touching a wisp of Charlotte's long curls. "Hers was light brown, like yours."

"Really?"

The expression on Charlotte's face was stupid. She looked like someone had given her a present. Mom had the same look. Dreamy-eyed. Christy frowned, making sure her face didn't look like that. She reminded herself that this man was pushing her out of her own bedroom. Thinking that, it was easy to resent him.

"Charlotte, why don't you take Mr. Palmer to his room."

"Ethan," he turned and said. "I'd like it if you'd all call me that."

"All right," Mom agreed, "Ethan."

Christy watched him climb the stairs, a suitcase in each hand. He was easy to look at—Mom

188

wasn't wrong about his being handsome—but there was something about him. Was it the way he glanced back down the stairs at Christy? What was that prying glance supposed to mean? As if he were staring into her.

She felt as if her house had been invaded. The enemy had moved in, and she was trapped.

You can become a member of

We dare you to join THE NIGHT-MARE CLUB...and receive your special member's packet including your membership card, THE NIGHTMARE CLUB Newsletter, a poster of THE NIGHTMARE CLUB insignia, auto-graphed photos of the authors, and other exciting gifts.

To join, send your name and address to:

**The Nightmare Club
Membership Dept.
Z*Fave Books
475 Park Avenue South
New York, NY 10016**

Please allow 6—8 weeks for delivery.
Quantities limited. Offer good while supplies last.